Rosetta Otwell Cross

The Suffering Millions

Rosetta Otwell Cross

The Suffering Millions

ISBN/EAN: 9783743422407

Manufactured in Europe, USA, Canada, Australia, Japa

Cover: Foto ©Andreas Hilbeck / pixelio.de

Manufactured and distributed by brebook publishing software (www.brebook.com)

Rosetta Otwell Cross

The Suffering Millions

THE

Suffering Millions

By ROSETTA OTWELL CROSS.

EDITED BY A GRADUATE OF THE UNIVERSITY OF MICHIGAN.

ANN ARBOR, MICH.:

THE COURIER OFFICE, PRINTERS.

1890.

PREFACE.

THE author, after a painful observation of more than a quarter of a century, was drawn to write this sad story, hoping by the sale of the book to help educate and elevate the children of unworthy parents. Those of us who enjoy comfortable homes, finding father and mother but synonyms of love and protection, can hardly be brought to realize what demons in human garb stalk through the homes of some of the children of the land.

Rev. T. Dewitt Talmadge, in one of his sermons, said: "The children of besotted parents are worse off than the orphan. Look at the pale cheek, woe bleached it. Look at that gash across the forehead, a drunken father struck it there. Hear that heart-piercing cry, a fallen mother's blasphemy compelled it. The ranks of an army of neglected children are being filled up from all the homes of iniquity and shame. The death-knell has already begun to toll, and the angels of God hover like birds over the plunge of a cataract. While such children are on the brink they halt, and throw out their hands, and cry: 'help! help!' O. Church of God, will you help?"

As the author of this very sad story, I feel to make an apology. No doubt my readers will think me cold and cruel, and possessing no true respect for a *mother*. But, indeed, such is not the case. My own dear mother's image is fresh in my mind, although many years have passed since she died, I remember her with a sweet smile and a soft, cheerful voice. I now remember standing by her side and listening to her tender, earnest reproof. Me-

4 *Preface.*

thinks I can now see her loving face, and it is because I
saw almost perfection in her that I realize the *importance
of a mother's God-given work*—yet few, comparatively, seem
to realize the importance of their mission. And now while
darling little ones play around *my own* door, I fully realize
my important duty. Oh, may I have mind and strength
to perform my task aright. But yet my heart bleeds, not
for Lulu Montroville alone, but for the thousands of helpless
children in homes illy kept, who have no kind relative to
raise them from sorrow and disgrace; without one ray of
encouragement to battle with the trials of life. "Ah, yes,"
says one, " Where there is a will there is a way." But
tell me, pray, where is the way for the child of a dissipated
parent, who barely provides bread? How can the child
who has no early advantages, who has to wrestle with poverty and want, besides having a parent who by life and
conduct daily drags his children down, be expected to have
the knowledge and the will-power necessary to succeed in
an attempt to elevate himself from the position in which
he is by such circumstances placed. Hard, indeed, it is
for a youth to be pointed out as the son of a drunkard,
or the daughter of a mother of *disgraceful character*. Although sad, yet it is nevertheless true, that there are many
children who have both sides of this question to face.
Methinks I can almost feel their little hearts beat, and see
the tears trickle down their cheeks, while they are surrounded by the children of worthy parents who have more
than they need.

CHAPTER I.

Whilst I alone did call upon thy aid,
    My verse alone had all thy gentle grace;
But now my gracious numbers are decay'd
    And my sick muse doth give another place.
I grant, sweet love, thy lovely argument
    Deserves the travail of a worthier pen;
Yet what of thee thy poet doth invent,
    He robs thee of, and pays it thee again,
He lends thee virtue, and he stole that word
    From thy behavior; beauty doth he give,
And found it in thy cheek; he can afford
    No praise to thee but what in thee doth live,
Then, thank him not for that which he doth say
    Since what he owes thee, thou thyself dost pay.
                                —*Shakespeare.*

In some way, my mind has to-day wandered back to a visit I made many years ago. At that time my health was quite poor, and I had been trying the air of different countries. I happened to meet an old acquaintance once or twice with whom I spent a short time.

"Well," said Mr. Bradberry, a gentleman at whose house I was visiting, "there are some new comers that have moved into our neighborhood, would you not like to go with wife and I this afternoon and call upon them?"

" I think no doubt it would be pleasant to do so," said I.

After dinner Mr. Bradberry said to his sons, " saddle the horses, and we will call upon our new neighbors."

As we were on our way, Mr. Bradberry said, "in some way I feel a peculiar interest in Mr. Montroville, which, by the way, is our new neighbor's name."

As we came in sight of the residence, which I saw to be newly built, I observed that there was only a small clearing around the house. As we drew near a gentlemanly-looking man came out of the house to meet us.

" Good afternoon, Mr. Bradberry," said he, " glad to see you. Will you not alight from your horses?"

" I think we will," said Mr. Bradberry. " We have a friend visiting us whom I thought you might be glad to meet."

" Indeed," said Mr. Montroville, " we will be glad to form new acquaintances, as we are very lonely in our new home."

" Well," said Mr. Bradberry, turning to me, " this is Miss Atwood, an intimate friend of my wife."

" Glad to meet you," said Mr. Montroville, ": come now into the house."

After being made acquainted with the family, Mr. Bradberry said, " well, friend Montroville, you seem to be very pleasantly situated in your new home."

At this remark of Mr. Bradberry's I saw the color mount to Mr. Montroville's face.

"Well," said he, "we try to make it as pleasant as possible."

I now noticed what a fine, noble, and intelligent looking man he was. I at once read in his looks that he had known better days, and that he was somewhat embarrassed at his surroundings. Mrs. Montroville appeared more at ease. She seemed to be a good-hearted woman, but I was somewhat amused at her peculiar vocabulary. Although strange to me, yet I knew it must be her native dialect.

"By the way," said Mr. Bradberry, "I met a man the other day that had known you years ago."

"Indeed," said Mr. Montroville, who could he have been, and why did he not come to see me?"

"Oh!" said Mr. Bradberry, "it was when I was in Cincinnati. I believe he called his name Bryant."

"Oh! indeed, was it he?" said Mr. Montroville.

"He seemed very much astonished to hear you were living here."

"I suppose he was," said Mr. Montroville.

"He thought," said Mr. Bradberry, "you were in a far away country."

"Well," said Mr. Montroville, "when I last saw him I was in far different circumstances."

"So he told me," said Mr. Bradberry.

"When I sold my property it was my intention

to go to another country," was the reply. "Little did I think I should ever come to this. But there arose against it, as it were, a tempestuous wind. No doubt if I had gone I would now have been well situated."

. "Perhaps," said Mr. Bradberry, "the winds were God's messengers."

"No, indeed, rather do I believe they were the messengers of the evil one."

"But," said Mr. Bradberry, "God does not wish us to despair."

"Well," replied Mr. Montroville, "how easy it is to be cheerful in the sunlight. How hard it is to be bright in a dark day. No, indeed, God's messengers never brought me here. Everything has gone wrong with me since I came here. No, the dear messengers of God, I do believe, did at one time call me to labor in his vineyard, but I heeded not the call."

"Why did you not do as God commanded you?"

"Well, I must acknowledge my mind was drawn away by the vanities of the world—I, being somewhat ambitious to gain wealth and a position in the world so I might better provide for my children. But now I fully realize the change has been one that will involve my family in sorrow and suffering."

"Why do you thus think?"

"I fully understand now, that it was unfaithfulness on my part not to heed God's call. No, I can now never view the promised land that my blessed Savior had intended me to enjoy."

I saw in his noble face a look of dispair, a wasted talent, one of God's best gifts to man. I very much feared he was as was one of old: Matt. 25 chap. 25 v.: "And I was afraid and went and hid thy talent in the earth: Lo! there thou hast. that is thine." Matt. 25–26:—"For unto every one that hath shall be given, and he shall have abundance; but from him that hath not, shall be taken away even that which he hath."

Shortly after our arrival a lady came in from another room, whom Mrs. Montroville introduced as Mrs. Lovejoy, and whom we soon found out was an old acquaintance of the family. As my curiosity was aroused I was quite anxious to learn something about the former circumstances of Mr. Montroville and his family.

While Mrs. Montroville was busily engaged in making some arrangements for tea, Mrs. Lovejoy said, "I have known Mr. Montroville's family for many years. At one time," said she, "Mr. Montroville was quite wealthy, having farms, horses, and cattle, and enjoying more of the luxuries of life than were common in that early day, but he finally became interested in speculation which wrought his financial ruin. Since that time he has never been the same man."

"Well," said Mrs. Bradberry, "I think it best for men who are comfortably situated to let well enough alone."

" Yes," said Mrs. Lovejoy, " I know it is, yet you know people do not all think so."

Just then Mrs. Montroville came in and invited us to tea. Shortly after this we took our departure. But I had become so much interested in the family that I made up my mind I would learn more about them.

CHAPTER II.

There was a "logging" at Mr. Sherman's. These were common at this time. Men would invite their neighbors to help in rolling logs into large heaps, in order to clear up the land. For the boys and young men these were great places for sport.

"Hurrah," said Bill Lawton, "now for some fun. We now ken see, arter all, who is the smartest man. Whoa! gee! hawe! you poor old critter," said he to his large red oxen, which he felt very proud of, although trying to pretend to the contrary. They were the finest yoke of oxen in the whole country, and considered in this early day, as a very valuable piece of property. Now, Bill was a good-hearted fellow, according to his light, which, however, was not great, yet he deemed it very smart to talk loud, boistrous and commanding to his faithful oxen. "Wal. boys," said he, "ef I was you I would begin showin' what I could do; jest fly in. S'pose, I reckon, you are thinkin' 'bout the gals. Jest let 'em alone till we get all of these logs together, then to-night at the kissin' bee, you can do all of the smilin' on the gals you wan' to, which ain't railly any fun for me; but laws a massy, I can remember when I, arter all, liked to smack a purtty gal's lips middlin' well. I dunno that there is any harm in it, mebby arter all it kindy cheers a fellow up once in a while."

At this speech of Bill Lawton, there was a shout of "hip, hip, hurrah!" by a dozen or more boys who were wild with the love of sport.

"Now, Bill," said one, "if you do not mind, Fred Brown's oxen will do more work than yours."

"Not much, Whoa, gee, hawe, Buck and Bright," said Bill, "Arter all, not wantin' to brag on these critters, ef any one thinks they have a yoke that can do half as much work I would like to see them. 'Mazin' strange, 'mazin' strange how much they can do." The shouts of the boys made the woods ring with the melody of their voices. "Whoa, gee, hawe," said Bill, as he rolled together one or two of the largest logs.

As the dinner horn sounded there was a general rush of the hungry men and boys for the house, and after washing the coal and dust from their hands and faces they gathered around the dinner table.

"Well," said Billy Lawton, "I s'pose you all know who done the most loggin'; bimby, I reckon, you know who'll do the most at the table."

"Well," said Captain Carlton, a man of action as well as thought, "Bill, I suppose you are capable of doing justice to both."

"I reckon so," said Bill as he handed his cup for some more coffee.

"By the way," said young Preston, "have any of you heard of the marriage?"

"The marriage!" said Carlton, "Who is married?"

"Have you not heard of it? Why, William Montroville has taken unto himself a wife."

"Laws a massy! do tell! did I ever!" said Bill Lawton, "Will Montroville, married! Why, he is only a young boy!"

"Yes," said Preston, "only seventeen."

"What a pity," said Captain Carlton. "Will is entirely too young to get married. Who did he marry?"

"He married Jane Winters."

"For mercy sakes," said Carlton, "worse and worse. How did he get acquainted with her?"

"Oh! he met her at a party and in just twenty-six days afterwards they were married. She just infatuated the boy. You know she is the older of the two."

"Well," said Capt. Carlton, "This surely is too bad. William would have made a fine young man had he remained single."

"Laws a Massy!" said Bill Lawton, "Jane belongs to a good family, arter all."

"I don't care if she does," said Carlton, "She is no wife for him."

"'Mazin' strange! 'mazin' strange," said Bill, "You think so little of Jane."

"Well," said Carlton, "Nothing could be more effectual than educating the future mothers for the advancement of the people."

" Wal," said Bill, "Jane larnt some eddication."

" Well," said Carlton, " She has not been properly educated, besides, she is not a fit person for any one to marry."

" Do tell! Laws a massy! She belongs to a good family," said Bill.

" I don't care if she does, I think wisdom should dictate the person and not the family; besides you just remember," said Carlton, " this marriage will turn out bad. Beside, Will is too young."

"Arter all, I dunno, Peggie and I were married young. I had nothin' at the beginin', and nothin' much yit. Mebby if we had staid single, and as you say got some eddication, it mite of ben better. But arter all I and the old gal has got along middlin well."

" I suppose you will think me a Philomath," replied Carlton, " but nevertheless I do love education. Why did Mr. Montroville let him marry so young, and on such short acquaintance ? "

" Well," said Mr. Sherman, " since Mr. Montroville met with his reverse in fortune he has never been the same man. He knew nothing of the marriage until one or two days before it took place. He then talked to William and the boy threatened to run away. This Mr. Montroville could not stand. He just idolized William, and has always indulged him very much."

" Poor boy," said Capt. Carlton, " he will regret this hasty step. Just remember if my words are not true."

"Another cup of coffee," said Bill Lawton, "Carlton has made me nervous. Nothin' jist like coffee, I reckon, ken quiet the nerves. S'pose ef we don't hurry we hain't goin' to git that piece of ground logged off. I railly 'spect, arter all, the boys begin to git scar't about the frolick to-night. Mrs. Sherman, another cup of coffee, I see my cup has run dry agin." Now, Bill was a good hearted fellow, was very fond of coffee, and thought it nothing, especially at a logging bee, to drink four or five cups to stimulate his nerves. But nevertheless this tickled the girls who were waiting on the table, they would insist upon Bill's having more coffee, winking at each other. Finally Mr. Sherman noticed their fun and gave his daughter a frown that made her plainly understand that he wished their sport stopped at once, for Bill Lawton was a good, hard working man, and welcome to all the coffee he wished. Coffee was a very important beverage in those good old days, especially for such fellows as Bill.

"Marriage," observed Capt. Carlton, "is a very important step. An eminent man once said that people should pray more over their marriage for God's assistance to direct them, than any other step in life, as it is the one of the most importance."

"Laws a massy!" said Bill, "I jest s'pose ef arter all they would use a little common sense, sich amount of prayin' railly ain't of no use. I reckon ef a person is a middlin' weak-minded fel-

low prayin' might ease his mind. 'Mazin' strange
how some people think."

" Well," said Mrs. Sherman, " Friend Lawton,"
as she helped him to another cup of coffee, " marriage is a very important step, and one that a person should ask God's guidance in, for, as Capt.
Carlton says, it is the most important step of a
worldly nature. I once knew a girl, a bright intelligent girl, that had been as well educated as any
girl in the whole country around where she lived."

" Do tell," said Bill, " wasn't that right?"

". Yes, but I was going to say, she became acquainted with a young man that was uneducated.
Being very handsome he soon won the girl's heart.
She being an orphan and feeling very lonely, very
much needed some one to lean upon. He was
constantly by her side, her every wish he tried to
grant and soon became all the world to her. She
gave the subject of the difference in their education no thought. She looked upon him as the best
and most handsome man she ever saw. Her
mind was fairly crazed with the love she felt for
him. Led on by her foolish love she became his
wife, never once thinking that they were entirely
unsuited for each other."

" Wal arter all I reckon the gal was happy, was
she not?" said Bill.

" Yes, for a number of years she was, but her
cultured mind longed and craved cultured society.
This I discovered although she tried to keep it to

herself. She was my nearest and dearest friend. As the beauty of youth wore away, leaving his mind unstored with knowledge, the difference became more apparent. This she could not help seeing, but being a true woman there was no other way, but to try and bear this mortification."

After dinner the men were soon engaged again in rolling the logs together. I noticed a number of other men and boys had come in to help Mr. Sherman during the afternoon. Among the number I noticed William Montroville. At the supper table, I could not help watching him as I had heard the conversation at noon about his marriage. I was touched with a feeling of sorrow, as I watched the youthful one. William was rather a heavy built boy. I must call him a boy, as surely that was all he was. His hair was a rich dark auburn, which lay in wavy curls around his noble brow.

"For mercy sakes," said Mrs. Sherman, "why did Mr. Montroville let a boy so young get married?"

I replied, "That is more than I can tell."

"He surely indulged William too much."

"Yes, he just idolized the boy."

"Well," said Mrs. Sherman, "Spare the rod, and you spoil the child. But in these days parents let the children govern the household. Is it not a pity?"

Capt. Carlton turned to William, whom he

2

watched with a tender, fatherly look, "How did your father make it with Mr. B. about those mules he let him have?"

"Oh!" said William, "Mr. B. would not change back."

"Well," said Carlton, "he did not act right, did he?"

"No, he did not. I had a very peculiar dream last night about Mr. B. and those mules."   .

"What was it?"

"I dreamed I was going up a high hill, over a very hard, stony road. I thought I heard a noise behind me, and upon looking around, I saw Mr. B.'s father-in-law coming, standing up in his wagon, driving those mules just as fast as he could. When, lo and behold! Just as Bunyan described Christian with that great burden on his back, so likewise he had Mr. B. secreted on his back trying in this way, as I dreamed, to get him into heaven."

At this witty sally of William's a hearty laugh went round.

"Well." said Lawton, "Ef he ever gits thare, I s'pose that is the only way for him, bekase he is too mean to git thare any other way."

"Friend Lawton you are most too hard on Mr. B.," said Carlton. "You know, ' while the lamp holds out to burn, the vilest sinner may return.'"

Turning to me, Mrs. Sherman said, "William Montroville is the most witty boy I ever saw. He is always full of fun and his fun is usually very

innocent. But you see Mr. B. took advantage, in
some way, of Mr. Montroville about those mules,
therefore William has been rather cutting in his
remarks."

"Well," said Bill Lawton, "gist good enough
for him. Old B. is always doin' somethin' he had-
ent orto. Ef I was in Montroville's place I'd give
him a good thrashin'. That's gist what he needs.
That Bill Montroville is gist the right kind of
stuff. Bimby ef B. don't look out he may be sorry
yit for some of his mean tricks, bekase some day
he will run across the wrong feller, and ef he does
he'll git it."

In the evening all of the young people of the
neighborhood gathered. The odor of wild flowers
filled the house. Girls and boys both, with ruddy
cheeks and sparkling eyes, presented perfect em-
blems of health. Oh, youth and health! what
are like thee? I some times now sigh for those
good old days of yore. It was not long before the
young folks were whirling in the giddy mazes of
the dance.

A short time after this logging bee I engaged
board for three or four months at the home of Mr.
Montroville. I had intended to board during the
fall and winter with my friend Mr. Bradbury, but
as it was impossible for them to accommodate me,
and there were very few places in this early day
where a person could secure board, I had to be
satisfied in doing the best I could in securing a

boarding place. But I felt a change in scenery and climate would be beneficial to my health.

In the family there were three children, two boys and one girl; the girl being the youngest of the family. The boys names were William and Ward, which were their true names. The girl we will call May. This family were very happy in their home, while prosperity was theirs to enjoy. The mother, Mrs. Montroville, was one of those good gentlewomen who indulged her children in almost their every desire. She was a good, kind and loving mother. Mr. Montroville was a man of government who tried to instruct his children in the way that they should go. Things passed pleasantly along until Mr. Montroville invested in some speculation that wrought his financial ruin. We now find them as the reverse of fortune always leaves people, in changed circumstances. Mr. Montroville being proud and ambitious was crushed at leaving his fine home, went to a city to live. But that did not suit the family, as the ways of city life were different from what they had been used to. Mr. Montroville also saw that the city was no place for his boys, he therefore took the means he had left, and bought him a home in the then wilds of southern Michigan. Mrs. Montro-ville and May remained in the city while Mr. Montroville, William and Ward went into the wild forest to make a home. Mr. Montroville hired a carpenter to build him a house, which, when completed, was quite a respectable frame house. Mr. Montroville and the boys began the hard task of clearing up a farm. The great and lofty trees that towered away up toward the heavens looked like giants and almost disheartened Mr. Montroville as he had not been used to such work. But, as man was to go forth and subdue the earth, they labored on, and as industry and perseverance will accomplish all things so in this case it was not long before they had cleared from the forest quite a farm. The boys enjoyed the sports of a new country. There was plenty of game in the woods, and the boys when they had time would hunt the game common to the country. Mr. Montroville bought the boys a large hound to hunt with which amused them very much. William was the oldest of the children, he therefore felt the reverse of their circumstances the most. Ward was a very bright, active boy that enjoyed the fine scenery of the woods. While in the city he had attended some of the great caravans that traveled about the world, and he there saw the fine bare-back riders and show men expert in riding horses in every imaginable way. He there-fore gained a love for that fine sport, and though but a boy of thirteen years yet he became very expert as a horse trainer. He would ride a horse as fast as it could run, while standing on its back. He was so active he could do almost anything in the line of climbing a tree, or riding a horse. He

could climb a tree almost equal to a squirrel. He
would almost run from the bottom to the top of
great tall trees. He was looked upon by the people as almost a clown. Many were the hardships
the family had to encounter, but as industry and
activity always bring happiness, they were happy
in their new home. There are many pleasures
in a new region that the people of an older and
more improved country know nothing of. The
people were warm-hearted and kind, as is almost
always the case in a new country. In older and
more improved countries the people become
more formal. One sad affliction was, that the
boys had not the opportunity of attending school,
as it was impossible for their father to spare
them, as he had so much work to do and was
not able to hire help. This was a very great
pity, as youth is the time to improve the mind
for future usefulness. We will here remark
that one of the greatest mistakes of life is
not to educate children. Although these boys
grew to be smart and intelligent men; with more
than ordinary capacity of mind; yet they never
could attain the same usefulness in life that they
might and that they would have been so well able
to have filled. But nevertheless they grew to be
noble and good men. With May the circumstances were different. Mrs. Montroville was a
healthy, industrious woman that took all of the
household care upon herself. The family being

small she did not need the services of May very much; and being the youngest, and the only girl she indulged the child very much. May therefore had the advantage of attending school as much as she wished. For a new country the school advantages were very good. Among the leading citizens were a family* of Puritans, descendants of the noble settlers of Plymouth Rock. They were cultured and educated people. This was a great help to the neighborhood for they did much to improve and elevate the people. They secured fine and able eastern teachers, to the great advantage of the schools, and for a new country the school advantages were better than are generally found. May at first felt very bashful to go to school alone, without her brothers. It was some time before she felt easy and contented in a strange school, but as she became acquainted with the scholars her bashfulness wore away. She soon began to enjoy the school, and being bright and intelligent she soon made rapid progress in her studies. The school house was one mile from her home. The road about half way was through the woods, fine large trees shading it on either side. There also ran a beautiful stream of water over which she had to pass.

Mrs. Montroville was of southern blood, born and raised in the south. Her people were slaveholders, and she therefore possessed much of the disposition of southern folks. She did not like the hardships of the working class of people, and ever sighed for her southern home. She had been brought up as the people of the south were, at that time, to believe in slavery. She had received but little education and used many of the southern terms of speech. Although gentle herself, yet her children partook largely of the fiery and ambitious nature of the southern people. Mr. Montroville also was of southern descent, although born and raised in the north. But his disposition was much as the disposition of southern people are, therefore this family felt much the change of their loss of property, but they tried to make the best out of life they could, they labored hard to make a home in the woods.

CHAPTER III.

Said Mr. Montroville to his wife, " I very much fear there is going to be trouble about the slave question. To-day, while 1 was in town, every-thing was excitement. You know there has been hard feelings by many because Mr. Douglas was not elected. On the occasion of Mr. Lincoln's inauguration he delivered a long and thoughtful address, declaring his fixed purpose to uphold the Constitution, enforce the laws, and preserve the integrity of the Union."

" Well," said Mrs. Montroville, " I suppose that is right, is it not ? "

" Of course it is," said Mr. Montroville, " but you know there has been hard feeling for a long time about the slave question."

" Well," said Mrs. Montroville, " they had better let the slaves remain just where they are, for I do believe that the slaves in my father's kitchen were better off than are the poorer class of people here in the north."

" Yes, but I hold these truths to be self evident, that all men are created equal; that they are en-dowed by their Creator with certain inalienable rights ; that among these are life, liberty, and the pursuit of happiness."

" Then they had better let the negroes be just where they are, for they are the happiest people I ever saw. I have heard them sing and dance, and shout, and have more fun in one night, than I have ever seen any one have in all of the time I have been in the cold, frozen north. The people of the north do not understand their natures, and that they are free from care. There was Uncle Nathan Chaffin's slaves. They were ten times better off than half of the poorer working class of the north."

" No doubt some were, but if they happened to have such a Master as old Legree, in Uncle Tom's Cabin, then what ? "

" Well, I know," said Mrs. Montroville. " Such men as he. is what makes slavery bad, yes, very bad, indeed. Of course there are some brutes in the form of men, who are very mean to their slaves."

" I shall go to town to-morrow to get my paper said Mr. Montroville, then I can find out what they are doing down south. Also who the new cabinet are."

The next evening. as the family were seated around the fire, Mr. Montroville read that the new cabinet was organized with W. H. Seward, of New York as secretary of State; Salmon P. Chase, of Ohio, secretary of the treasury ; and Simon Cameron, secretary of war, (who in the following January was succeeded in office by Edwin M.

Stanton). The secretaryship of the navy was conferred on Gideon Welles.

"I hope he has made a wise choice for his cabinet," remarked Mr. Montroville. In his inaugural address the President indicated the policy of the new administration by declaring his purpose to repossess the forts, arsenals and public property which had been seized by the Confederate authorities. On the 12th of March an effort was made by commissioners of the seceded states to obtain from the national government a recognition of their independence.

"No doubt this will be best for the north as well as for the south, said Mrs. Montroville."

"No, indeed," said Mr. Montroville. "Prudence will dictate that governments long established should not be changed for light and trivial causes. All experience hath shown that mankind are more disposed to suffer, while evils are sufferable, than to right themselves by abolishing the former to which they are accustomed."

"Ah!" said Mrs. Montroville, "I was raised in the south. I think I have a better right to know about it than you do. We had better times there than I ever expect to have here in the north."

"No doubt you did at the expense of some one else's labor." Just here Mr. Smith came in. Said he to Mr. Montroville, "I suppose you have heard of the trouble down south?"

"No," said Mr. Montroville.

" Well," said Mr. Smith, "you know the defences of Charleston Harbor were held by Major Robert Anderson. His entire forces amounted to seventy-nine men. Owing to the weakness of his garrison, he deemed it prudent to evacuate Fort Moultrie and retire to Fort Sumpter. In the meantime Confederate volunteers had flocked to the city and powerful batteries had been built about the harbor. As soon as it became known that the Federal government would reinforce the forts, the authorities of the Confederate States determined to anticipate the movement by compelling Anderson to surrender. Accordingly, General Beauregard, commandant of Charleston, sent a flag to Fort Sumpter demanding an evacuation. Major Anderson replied that he should hold the fortress and defend his flag."

"That was right," said Mr. Montroville, " it showed him to be a brave man."

Mr. Smith continued, " on the following morning the first gun was fired from a Confederate battery. A terrific bombardment of thirty-four hours' duration followed ; the fort was reduced to ruins, set on fire, and obliged to capitulate. The honors of war were granted to Anderson and his men, who had made a brave and obstinate resistance."

" Just as I expected. With this begins actual hostilities. I am very sorry indeed. This is going to make a bloody war. It will not be as many of

the northern men think. I well understand
the disposition of those southern people; they will
fight until they die. It is as brother against
brother. Many of my relations are in the south.
Yes, indeed, I am very, very sorry. How many
lives were lost?"

"There were no lives lost, but the fort was
ruined," replied Mr. Smith.

The news of this startling event went through
the country like a flame of fire. There had been
expectation of violence, but the actual shock came
like a clap of thunder. Public opinion in both
the north and south was rapidly consolidated.
Three days after the fall of Sumpter, President
Lincoln issued a call for seventy five thousand
volunteers to serve three months in the overthrow
of the secession movement. But, as Mr. Montroville feared, the war did not stop there, but continued to be a long and bloody one. On the 19th
of April, when the first regiment of Massachusetts
volunteers were passing through Baltimore on
their way to Washington, they were fired upon
by the citizens, and three men killed. This was
the first blood shed in the war.

Virginia seceded from the Union. On May 6th,
Arkansas followed, then North Carolina on the
20th of the same month. In Tennessee—especially
in East Tennessee—there was a powerful opposi-
tion to disunion, and it was not until the 8th of
June that a secession ordinance could be passed.

The people of Maryland were divided into hostile parties. In Missouri, the movement resulted in civil war. In Kentucky the authorities issued a proclamation of neutrality. Already the Southern Congress had adjourned from Montgomery, to meet on the 20th of July at Richmond, which was chosen as the capitol of the Confederacy. To that place had already come Jefferson Davis and the officers of his cabinet, for the purpose of directing the affairs of government and the army. So stood the anatagonistic-power in the beginning of June, 1861, and before the close of this year ten states had seceded from the Union. It was now evident that a great war, perhaps the greatest in modern times, was impending over the nation. "What do you think were the causes of the civil war?"

"Well," replied Mr. Montroville, "the first and most general cause of the war, was the different construction put upon the national constitution by the people of the north and south."

"Do you think this the greatest cause, said I?"

"No. A second general cause of the civil war was the different systems of labor in the north and in the south. In the former section the laborers were freemen, citizens, voters; in the latter, bondmen, property, slaves."

"Your wife, Mr. Montroville, seems to believe in slavery."

"Oh yes! You see my wife was born and raised in the south. Her best days were spent there.

She knew nothing but happiness there, so it is no wonder she believes in it. I, too, am of southern descent, yet I believe in abiding, by the laws of my country."

" That is right," said I.

" In the south," said Mr. Montroville, the theory was that the capital of a country should own the labor. In the north that both labor and capital are free. Thus there came to be a dividing line drawn through the Union, east and west."

" Were these the only causes ? "

" No. The danger arising from this source was increased, and the discord between the sections aggravated by several subordinate causes. The first of these was the invention of the cotton gin, in 1793, by Eli Whitney, a young collegian of Massachusetts. He went to Georgia, and while there his attention was directed to the tedious and difficult process of picking cotton by hand, that is in separating the seed from the fibre. The industry of the cotton growing states was paralyzed by the tediousness of preparing the product for the market."

" It must have been very tedious."

" It was, and young Whitney undertook to remove the difficulty, and succeeded in inventing a gin which astonished the beholder by the rapidity and excellence of its work."

" Surely this could have had nothing to do with the war ? "

" Well," said Mr. Montroville, " from being profit-
less, cotton became the most profitable of all the
staples. The industry of the south was revolution-
ized. Before the war it was estimated that Whitney's gin had added a thousand millions of dollars
to the revenues of the southern states. Slave
labor became important, slaves valuable, and the
system of slavery, a fixed and deep rooted institution."

" Well," said I, " It would not have been so bad,
had it not been for such brutes as Legree."

" Of course it would not, yet, no doubt many a
man has lost his soul on account of slavery,
and what can be compared to the worth of one
soul. From this time onward there was constant
danger that the slavery question would so embitter
the politics and legislation of the country as to
bring about disunion. The danger of such a result
was manifested in the Missouri agitation of 1820–
21. Next came the Nullification acts of south
Carolina. But still I love the south, for it was
the land of my parents' nativity. I also love the
north for it is my home. The place where my
children were born."

Thus sang a poor old colored woman at the beginning of the trouble down south :

> Ah! Praise and t'anks de Lo'd.
> He comes to set de people free,
> And Massa t'inks it day ob doom, but we of jubilee.

Ah ! poor ole Dinnah is afe'rd de Lo'd will let

you sing and shout de year of jubilee, 'spesually ob bein' free. Dis chile haint one ob de kind dat belibes in sich po'er ob de Lo'd ; bekase ef de Lo'd had ben so mighty good he wou'dn't let dem sold my poor wife and chile.

" Well," said Dinah, " now Sambo dare am foun' in de book of Solomen deze wo'ds, ' fo' dem dat sews de same shall they rip,' now de kashin ob my inter-ducin' dis subjec' am as wu'ked out en de las' meetin in dat dar grove."

" In de fust place," said Sambo, " I tuk notice dat 'mong de darkys de subjec' was bein' fabercated for de po'r headens, yo' look'd like a pack of po'r old fools don' on yo' shin bon's prayin' to be free. Fuddermo', an' in de nex' place lemme tell yo' dis, dat de Lo'd can no mor' do any t'ing 'bo't settin' yo' f'ee dan I can. Yo' gwinto see 'bo't dis, an' yo' kin ram dis truf down yo' t'ro't."

" Well, Sambo, Iz bin one ob de kind dat had conwictions dat de Lo'd is gwinter set us free. De Lo'd can take care of de babes ob de lam'."

" Well," said Sambo, as the tears flowed down his dusky cheeks, " why did de Lo'd den let dem sell my po'r wife an' den tare ou' po'r little chile from it mudder's bre'st ? De po'r little t'ing tried to cling to its mudder. Oh, de'r, ole massa is good, but de kinder de massa de harder to be sold. Dat it haint gwinto see de lubed ones any mor'. Day took my wife to Georgia to toil in de cotton

an' de cain. Day took ou' po' little babe, wh'ar
we can never see it agin."

> " We kno' de Lo'd he gib us sign,
>   Dat some day we be free;
>   De norf wind tell it to the pine,
>   De wild duck to de sea.
>   We t'ink it when de church bell rings,
>   We dream it in de dreams,
>   De rice bird means it when it sings,
>   De eagle when he screams."

CHAPTER IV.

As we have before made mention after associating for sometime among the young people, William
became acquainted with a young lady, whom he
shortly afterward married. Being yet very young
Mr. Montroville thought best for him to live at
home for a while, as their family was small, and
he did not like to spare one of the children from
the parental roof. William therefore brought his
wife home. Being much attached to his wife, also
to his father's family, he was very happy. Things
passed pleasantly along for some time. But about
this time there was a dark cloud hovering over our
beloved United States. Our nation was threatened with being disunited in heart and hand.
South Carolina had already seceded, Jefferson
Davis declaring that she was a free and independent State. It was then that our country called for
brave men. As a good father would try and
govern his household, so she saw something must
be done. She needed men to try and prevent disunion. William looked at his country's need, and
fired with the same warm blood that runs in southern veins, was ready and willing to go. Although
his friends were dear, yet duty called him now.
His country needed his help to protect the homes,

in one of which was all he held dear, that peace
might yet reign; and that children yet unborn
might enjoy the same liberty that he had ever
enjoyed. He bid wife, parents, brother and sister
adieu, and went at his country's call; if need be to
lay down his life, or to spill the last drop of blood
for freedom's sake. Sad was the parting. His
friends wrung their hands and wept, but they would
not hold him back, for they knew that duty called
him away. He was among the youngest and
bravest of northern men.

My health had so improved in this climate that
I made up my mind I would secure a regular
boarding place and remain for sometime. Mr.
Bradberry, whom I considered a very dear friend,
had enlarged his house, and now very kindly
offered me a home in his family. The Montrovilles
were not quite as comfortably situated, so I changed
my boarding place. But as I had become somewhat interested in the family I still kept up an acquaintance with them, partly on account of their
kindness towards me, and partly on account of
their peculiar temperaments. I was very much
affected at the parting of William and his friends,
yet I knew it was necessary that our country
should be protected.

" What bosom beats not *for* his country's cause
Briton's attend; be worth like this approved."—*Pope.*

Those were dark days for the people of this
country. Not like a war with a foreign nation, but

with brother against brother, both fighting as they thought, for their rights. Death and destruction invaded both armies. Blood flowed on many a battle field. The hearts of friends at home grew sad as they waited and longed for peace to be restored. But still the war swept on. A call was made for seventy-five thousand men. But even this number was too small, although more than the number of children of Israel that died with the plague in King David's time. Then again came a call for three hundred thousand more, and still again for three hundred thousand more. Then brave men rallied for the cause from Mississippi's winding stream, and from New England's shore, and still the war was continued. Starvation and all kinds of hardships, the soldiers in both armies endured. I speak of these sufferings to try and impress on the minds of the young and rising generations, and to those that know little or nothing of the sorrows of this dreadful war, what a bad thing it is for a nation to be divided and go to war, the one portion against the other. It is as " A house divided against itself shall not stand," and also, " Though the tongue is a little member it boasteth great things," yet it can " set nations on fire," therefore all should try and govern the tongue as well as the thoughts, for both used in the wrong direction can do great harm. It is my object in writing this volume to impress upon the mind of the young a right object in life, and the

great necessity of trusting God at all times, and in
all things, in little things as well as great.

After leaving home William met many trials
and temptations. Many are the wicked influences
thrown around a young man in the army. Although
almost overcome with grief at the parting with
friends and loved ones at home, after leaving
the north, and while in the south his mission was
to aid his beloved country. He made a brave and
gallant soldier. Although he loved the south and
the southern people, because it was his mother's
native land, yet he loved liberty and thought it
better for both north and south to be united, for
in unity there is strength. "United we stand
divided we fall," is a good maxim for either home
or country. Although away from home and friends,
and strange as it may seem, yet his brave and
dauntless nature enjoyed the wild and romantic
scenes of war. From his quick and active nature,
and possessing as he did the ability to imperson-
ate others, he acted many times as a spy. thereby
ofttimes doing more good to his country than he
could in any other capacity. He did not at this
time enjoy religion, therefore did not feel the
remorse of acting in such a capacity. The southern people were indignant at the northern soldiers,
and did all in their power to do them harm in
every way they could. There were many good
and loyal people in the south, which sometimes
made it hard to tell the loyal from the disloyal

ones. In one of the southern states lived a very rich, and influential man, who claimed to be loyal, but it was rumored that he was not loyal, and that he was helping the south in many ways, in furnishing provisions, and, also by acting as a spy, gaining knowledge of the northern army, and then communicating the same to the southern army. The union soldiers tried in many ways to find out whether he was really loyal or not. At last the officers of William's regiment conceived the plan of sending him as a spy. They therefore obtained a suit of southern planter's clothes, with broad rimmed hat, such as was worn by southern planters at that time, and William went to the old farmer's plantation, dressed as a young southerner. He well knew that if his identity was discovered death would be his immediate portion, because they do not parley long with one acting as a spy. Yet he was too brave to fear death, if by it he could aid his country, for this is what the truly brave soldier expected.

The old southern planter received him in truly southern style. After having him alight from his horse he had his servants bring out decanters of brandy, thereby showing his hospitality in true southern style. After conversing on different topics of the day, the old planter referred to "the d—d war" as he called it, which was ruining his country. He went on to tell how he had helped the confederate army, and stated that he had a son, an officer, in the rebel army. William asked him many questions in regard to the situation of the confederate army, and gained much information. As the old man was showing him his room up stairs William noticed the stars and stripes, our dear national flag, made into a bed quilt. If anything will make a loyal person's blood run cold, it is in seeing our beautiful flag mistreated. William stepped to the bed and raising the flag said, " You have the stars and stripes made into a quilt?"

" Yes," said the planter, " and a nicer one than that I dragged through the streets of Richmond, tied to my horse's tail."

This and many other things showed how loyal he was. At supper the planter's wife, more shrewd than her husband, a trait for which southern women were noted, looking over her spectacles, said to her husband, " you had better be a little careful of what you say, just as likely as not this young man is a union soldier."

" Not much," said the old man, " I guess I can tell a southern man's talk."

William was well acquainted with many of the southern phrases of speech, learning many of them years before of his mother, and they were very natural for him to use. In this way he had completely fooled the old planter. But this made William's blood run cold, for he well knew the result if he was found out. He remained with the planter until morning, and then excusing himself returned to the union army to relate how loyal the old gentleman was. His officers received him with warm congratulations for doing so brave and daring an act. One of the union Kentucky regiments seeing his bravery, and knowing him to possess southern blood, offered him an honorable position to serve with them, but his officers would not give him up. This he somewhat regretted, for he thought that he might be able there to better serve his country. We will leave him in the south, and return to his home in the far away north, with God's blessing upon him.

CHAPTER V.

We now come back to the home in the north. Sad, indeed, is the home of the soldier. While away, where death and hardship meets him on every hand, little can cheer the hearts of parents or wife as they wait, not knowing but the next mail may bring them tidings that will crush the heart and cause "an aching void that time can never fill." Mr. Montroville's family being so small, and so very lonesome, it was thought best for William's wife to remain with them, not only because of that fact but also because her father and mother were dead and she had no better place to stay. Things passed as pleasantly as could be expected. But there was soon to be a change that Mrs. Montroville and William's wife feared might cause trouble. May had always been the baby, never knowing the love of one younger than herself. She had been badly spoiled, and from being always indulged in having her own way, had become very selfish. She knew no government higher than her own. It is no kindness to a child to indulge it in a way that will cause it misery and sorrow all its life. This is one of the sins that will remain to the "third and fourth generation." God's laws were laws of government. He did not intend to make a law and then to have it broken. I have no patience with parents who will kneel down at a prayer meeting, or at any other public place, and pray for God to pour out his blessings upon their children, and then while at home let them do just as they please. Such prayers as these, in my candid opinion, do more harm than they do good. Worldly people point those Christians out and say, " Look at such a Christian's children ! They are the worst children in the neighborhood." Which is often the truth. It does more harm than this, for the Bible says, "Ask and ye shall receive," but it also says " God cannot lie," and it is not his plan to bless the raising of the children of parents, who let them act at home, here in an enlightened and a civilized land, worse than the children of parents in a heathen land. I have now in my mind a very devoted and saintly-appearing woman, who will kneel in public worship and ask God's blessing upon her children in the most eloquent language, and while at home allow those children to do all manner of wrong things. I do not believe that God looks upon such prayers with the least allowance. They put me in mind of the Pharisee who " loved to make long prayers in public to be seen of men." The Holy Bible says this is all they will receive. Their children should be pitied instead of being hated as they always are. The parents in their love of display in prayer, do not stop to think that

they are doing their children an injustice. Such
prayers are a shame and disgrace to the Christian
religion. · But one might say they have no faculty
to govern. But that is no excuse. We can cultivate our faculties if we try. If they have no faculty to govern, then let them "ask God in secret,
and he will reward them openly."

May's mother made no such prayers as these,
but she had always indulged her in having her
own way, and May was of a very impatient and
nervous temperament that made her very hard to
get along with. For this cause, Mrs. Montroville
feared that the change that was about to take
place might not make it as pleasant as it now was.
There was soon to come to that lonesome home
another little one. Many of the friends of William's wife said there would be trouble with May.
This they all feared, as William's wife was a
quarrelsome and inconsiderate woman. But when
the little stranger made its appearance May looked
upon it as a gem of unearthly sweetness. A new
joy had come to her heart and home. She had
never loved anything so well in all of her life
before. At first when she looked at it she felt
that she must cry. She thought of her brother far
away, for whom she had a very tender regard.
But as the little baby was happily a girl, May
made it the idol of her heart. It grew quite
rapidly, developing in sweetness day by day.
May had not much work to do, so she had much

time to spend with her little niece during her
vacations. Mrs. Montroville and William's wife
were will pleased, as might be expected, by the
way May received the little stranger. We will
call the baby Lulu, although this was not her true
name. Ward and Mr. Montroville also thought
the baby very nice. So many years had passed
since there had been a baby in the family that
the entire household received it with great joy.
As Lulu's mother was one of those idle women
who casts her burdens on some one else, Mrs.
Montroville had the care of little Lulu.

" Well, May," said I, " how do you like that
baby at your hou-e ? "

" Like that baby," said May, " Why, I just think
it splendid."

" Well," said I, " it is nothing remarkable, it is
only a baby."

" Only a baby ! Well I guess you never saw
one quite as nice as it is, did you ? "

" Pshaw ! there is Mrs. Harverland's, with beautiful brown hair, and those eyes ! I hope you
don't think your baby half so nice as that one is,
do you ? "

" Yes, I do," said May. " Mrs. Harverland's
baby is not pretty at all, just as homely as it can
be. Our baby has beautiful auburn hair, and I do
believe it is going to curl. Oh ! I do hope it will
be curly, for if it does, then it will be the prettiest
baby in the world. Did you notice its eyes ? They

are the prettiest, laughing, sparkling eyes I ever saw."

" Well, May," said I, "I should not think you could think so much of it. You have been the baby for fourteen or fifteen years. Now you will have to give all of your playthings to it. Besides, all of the new ones will be bought for it. You no longer are the baby, now you will have to stand back. You now are nothing but a great awkward girl."

" I don't care if I do. I never was half as nice as our baby is, nor do I think there ever was another half as sweet as she is. The other day when I went into the room where she was sleeping she opened her beautiful eyes and began to laugh, rubbing her little nose with her fist. I caught her in my arms and as I was kissing her she held on to my lips, sucking them until the blood nearly came."

" Well," said I, " I guess she wanted to punish you, by making your lips bleed for kissing her so."

" No, she didn't," said May. " She likes me. Mother says she never saw the like. She believes the baby likes me better than she does any of the rest. If anything goes wrong with her she will put up her little mouth and watch me all the while, and want to come to me."

" Oh! " said I, " she is making fun of you. She is nothing very nice, only a baby."

" Well, she is ten times nicer than you are," said May, as she left the room, slamming the door

after her. In a few minutes back she came. (I
now saw she had been thinking about our conversation, and had become angry at what I had been
saying about the baby.) "Well, said she, "I suppose you think that baby which belongs to your
family, I mean your aunt's baby, is nice?"

"Yes," said I, "I do."

"It looks just like a little nigger. It is black as
a stack of black cats," said May. "Our baby is
just like a snow-flake, white and pure and like a
lily fair."

"Oh!" said I, "you are getting poetical."

"I don't care how I am getting," said May.

"I am happy because we have got a baby at our
house. I never had a sister or a baby to play with
before. I always had to play with the boys,"
said she.

"That is why you are so rough and tom-boyish,"
said I.

"Perhaps, then," said May, "this dear, gentle,
angelic baby will help to make me more ladylike.
I have always had to play with my brothers. I
love their wild sports."

"Yes," said I, "but you are the worst of the
three. The other day as I passed you and your
brother Ward you were whipping your horse down
to the keen run. I heard Ward say, be careful,
May, you will get thrown, your horse is running·
I watched you until you went over the hill and
out of sight."

· " But, as I had the fastest horse, I left him far behind."

" Ward is just as mischievous as he can be," I said. " I noticed that he had two little American flags in his horse's bridle. I was glad to see that, for I do love a noble, patriotic spirit in our Amercan boys."

" Oh! yes," said May, " we love to trim up our horses to make them look nice, and as we were returning we passed young Crosby. I thought I would make a very favorable impression. But Ward gave my horse a cut with his whip, my horse gave a spring throwing me over its head, though I alighted on my feet the impression was a failure. He looked at us as if we were young Comanches."

" I should have thought he would," said I. " It is a great wonder you both do not get killed."

" Oh !" said May, " we are not as fraid of getting killed as you are. Don't you like to run horses? "

There would have been entire happiness in the family, had it not been for the loved one who was not there to enjoy the quiet and peace which reigned in that household. They watched the mail to hear from him and all were delighted by receiving letters. William wrote at every opportunity although it was somewhat difficult for him to write, as he had his two first fingers from his right hand shot off. Yet he did the best he could for he knew his friends were anxious to hear from

him. After one of the hard fought battles, that of
Atlanta, news came to Mr. Montroville that
William was mortally wounded. The grief they
endured was intense. They anxiously watched the
papers hoping to learn any information of the killed
and wounded. At last, joyful news came. A letter
from William stating that he had passed through
the battle safely, although many brave men had
fallen on that dreadful battle-field. War always
causes sadness and gloom over a bleeding country.
People always speak in honor of the brave men
who will lay down their lives for their country's
sake. Although we think war is not right, yet
when our country is invaded, or there is danger of
our beloved government, for which our forefathers
fought and bled that we might have free and
happy homes where we can worship God according to the dictates of our own consciences, none
to molest or make afraid, or when there is danger
of our beautiful stars and stripes being torn from
its lofty position and another emblem waving in
its stead, then the brave will come forth. And
although it is sad, yet it is noble, for our country
to die.

4

CHAPTER VI.

After four years of bloodshed, devastation, and sorrow, the Civil War in the United States was at an end. At the outbreak of the war the financial credit of the United States had sunk to a very low ebb. By the organization of the army and navy the expenses of the government were at once swelled to an enormous aggregate. At the presidential election in the autumn preceding the downfall of the confederacy, Mr. Lincoln was chosen president for a second term. As vice-president, Andrew Johnson, of Tennessee, was elected in place of Mr. Hamlin. On the 4th of March, 1865, President Lincoln was inaugurated for his second term. A month afterward the military power of the confederacy was broken. Three days after the evacuation of Richmond by Lee's army, the president visited that city, conferred with the authorities, and then returned to Washington.

Coming home one evening from town, there was a look of sorrow and anxiety on Mr. Montroville's face. Said he to his wife, " have you heard the sad news ?"

" No," was the reply, becoming somewhat excited."

" Well," said Mr. Montroville, " a disreputable
actor at Ford's Theatre, by the name of John
Wilkes Booth, stole unnoticed into the president's
box, leveled a pistol at the head of Mr. Lincoln,
and shot him through the brain."

" Why! for mercy sake!" exclaimed Mrs. Montroville.

" And killed the president, continued Mr. Montroville. " He lingered in an unconscious state
until the following morning and died."

" Oh, dear!" said Mrs. Montroville, " this is the
greatest tragedy of modern times."

" Yes, indeed," added Mr. Montroville, " the
most wicked, atrocious and diabolical murder
known in American history. And this was not all.
At the same hour another murderer, named Lewis
Payne Powell, burst into the bed-chamber of Secretary Seward, sprank upon his couch, and stabbed
him nigh unto death. The whole country is wild
with alarm and excitement. It is clear that a plot
was made to assassinate the leading members of
the government."

Mrs. Montroville then remarked: " This is very
bad indeed. What will they now do without a
president?"

" Oh!" was the reply, " on the day after the
assassination of Mr. Lincoln, Andrew Johnson, the
vice-president, took the oath of office, and became
president."

" Well," said Mrs. Montroville, " I fear he will

not fill Mr. Lincoln's place. He was born in Raleigh, North Carolina, you known that was my native state."

" Why do you think he will not fill Mr. Lincoln's place."

" Mrs. Montroville replied, " He had no early advantages of education, he passed his boyhood in poverty and neglect, and I have heard his relatives very badly spoken of. You see I had a chance to know something of him. He was born in 1808, one year after I was born."

" You must not judge too harshly, you know Mr. Lincoln also had many difficulties to encounter, but he was one of the most remarkable men of any age or country—a man in whom the qualities of genius and common-sense were strangely mingled. He was prudent, far-sighted and resolute."

" In 1826," said Mrs. Montroville, " Andrew Johnson removed with his mother to Greenville, Tennessee. Here he married an intelligent lady who taught him to write and cypher."

" Well," said Mr. Montroville, " by dint of native talent, force of will, and strength of character, he first earned the applause of his fellowmen, did he not?"

" Yes, but in someway, " said Mrs. Montroville, " I feel he is not the right man to fill such an important place, and I do believe all southern people would agree with me."

Said Mr. Montroville, "As a member of the U. S. Senate in 1861, he opposed secession with all of his zeal, even after the legislature had declared Tennessee out of the Union."

" I hope he will do well," was the reply.

" Well," said Mr. Montroville, " at least I think the lives of these two men, should be an encouragement to the young, they both have arisen from obscurity to the responsibilities of Chief Magistrate of these United States of America. I thank the great, living God that peace has been declared, continued he, and you know ' The darkest hour, is just before day.' "

After the close of the war the poor old woman that had such faith in the Lord, still clung to Providence.

" Well, Sambo," said Dinah, as she rolled the whites of here eyes heavenward, and while a smile wreathed her face, which showed her pearly teeth.

> "We kno'd de promise nebber fail,
>   Nor nebber lie de wo'd;
> So like de prisoner in de jail,
>   We waited for de Lo'd.
> An' now he open every door
>   An' t'row away de kee;
> He t'ink we lub him so before,
>   We lub him better free."

" T"anks de bless'd Lo'd," said Sambo, dis po' chile waz too ignorent to t'ink dat he could eber see poor ole wife an' chile, but one day looking out in de gloomerin' meadows, I seed som' one comin'. Who dat? said I. In jist one minute my po' ole wife throw'd herself into my arms. She had found our chile, when de massa told her she waz free, she at once came all de way, t'ro' night, rain and win' from Ole Georgia. You seed she kno'd whar to fin'.me, but dis chile den did not kno' whar to look fo' dem. Yes, bless de Lor'd ; Dey po' los' sheep ob de sheepfol', dey all comes gadderin' in."

" Yo' see, Sambo, de Lo'd nebber fail."

" Well," said Sambo, " dis chile am so blind, bekase he iz so mighty wick'd dat he could not at dat time hab faith. But bless de good Lo'd, he nebber fail."

" Oh! no," said Dinnah, " de dear Lo'd nebber fail, nor nebber lie de wo'd, if only like de prisoner in de jail, we have faith in his wo'd."

" Well," said Sambo, " I did think yo' lookt like a pack of poo' old fools, prayin' to be free, bekase I did not believe de Lo'd could do such a mighty thing."

" Ah!" replied poor old Dinnah, as she rolled the whites of her eyes heavenward, " did de dear Lo'd not lead de children thro' de Red Sea? Did he forsake Jacob when he wrestled all night? No, de dear Lo'd nebber lie de wo'd. De whole truble is in de weakness of de flesh, bekase we habe not de faith of mustard seed."

Brave men are always honored, while cowards

are always despised, even by the lower order of
animals, but much more so by the human family.
Even on a battle field the enemy will honor the
brave on either side, while cowards are held in
derision. The war of the Great Rebellion was a
very sad thing because it was as brother against
brother. But as children of one family often
quarrel and fight, still their love for each other is
intense. So in this war. But after the good Heavenly Father severely chastised both the north, as
well as the south, he then let the palm of peace
wave over our beloved country. And although
more than a score of years have passed away, yet
peace and prosperity still reigns. This was plainly
seen at the death of our late loved Martyr President, James A. Garfield. Both north and south
stood hand in hand, and wept the silent tear, and
may the blessing of an Allwise God still continue
to bless both, as they stand hand in hand. Although we were badly chastised, yet we should not
complain, for " whom the Lord loveth he chasten-
eth." It was a long and bloody war. Many loved
ones parted there to meet no more on earth, but
as William Montroville was not born to die on a
battle field, after passing through nineteen battles
and skirmishes, he was permitted to return home
after the war closed and peace was restored, with
an honorable discharge. He had been promoted
to an office sometime before the close of the war,
yet he always felt proud of being called a soldier,

for it was then that he did his work in restoring
the Union. Mr. Montroville's folks knew that
peace had been declared, but they did not know
just when William would be at home. But they
were anxiously expecting him. At last, unexpectedly to all, he came. He was so anxious to
get home, that he did not write to have any one
meet him at the station, near his father's, therefore he walked home from the train. It was just
about noon on a beautiful autumn day. So overcome was he with joy at meeting his loved ones
that at first he could not speak. He met his father
first and they clasped each other in their arms.
Ward, the younger brother, was some distance
from the house, but he knew him at a glance. He
made one or two bounds and in a moment had his
brother in his arms. Next came May, so delighted
was she at seeing her darling brother once more
that she almost smothered him with kisses. Then
came Mrs. Montroville, calm and quiet, but thank-
ing God, who had taken care of her boy through
an awful and bloody war and had permitted her to
see him once more. William's wife and Lulu were
away from home on a visit, therefore he did not
see them just then. The family were so delighted
and overcome with joy that a young lady visiting
at Mrs. Montroville's, an intimate friend of Ward
and May, especially of Ward, had to finish the
dinner that had already been begun. The boy
who went away, for William was not eighteen

years old, although he was married, had grown
into a man. Three long years of war, 'neath the
burning rays of a southern sun, had changed his
looks and had improved his manly form. But his
heart was just the same. In afterwards speaking
of their meeting, he said it effected him worse than
the battle's awful roar, because it so effected him
that he could not speak, and he had never been
effected in that manner before. After dinner May
was anxious to send for William's wife so that
he might see little Lulu, as he had never seen her,
she being born after he went away. Therefore
Ward went after them. They were only two or
three miles from home, so it did not take them
long. This, also, as might be expected, was a
happy meeting. William looked for the first time
on his lovely little daughter. Lulu had grown to
be a very lovely child. Her hair hung in wavy
ringlets around her head, with an angelic look on
her handsome face. Eyes so impressive that my
pen fails to describe them, and so gentle was she
in her nature—so different from May—and so
woman-like, that she always appeared just like a
little lady. William and his wife remained for
sometime at Mr. Montroville's, then he built him
a house near his father's and went to house-keep-
ing. Now that peace was restored things passed
along quietly, nothing of importance occurring for
some time. It was not far from William's to his
father's, so little Lulu could run back and forth as

much as she wished. She was always a welcome
guest at her grandpa's, a fact she well knew.
When she had been away for sometime she would
walk in triumphantly, clapping her little hands
and say, " Dranpa! I's dot home!" well knowing
that all were so delighted to have her there that
they could not bear to have her away. William
never forgot his days in the south. He delighted
to talk and dwell on them. He would often spend
the long winter evenings at his father's talking of
the dashing scenes of war. Although he did not
like to have people killed, yet there was something
about it that was animating to his nature. Mr.
Montroville made an idol of William. He could not
bear to have him away from his side. He seemed
to feast upon his society, as he was his first born.

CHAPTER VII.

After William went to housekeeping, his parents, and Ward and May were somewhat lonesome, but little Lulu visited them very often. Mrs. Montroville had some relics of her southern home, among them was a side-saddle, a gift from her father. In her day in the south it was fashionable for women to ride horse back. The southern people were a sport loving people. She often loved to tell of the gay times she had when a girl away down in the sunny south. She would tell of meeting with girls of her own age, then taking their fathers' race horses, and go, when they thought no one would see them, to the race paths where the men trained and ran their horses, and there try their skill at speeding them. This may not seem right to some, but in those days in the south things were looked upon differently than they are now. Nevertheless she enjoyed such sport, and as southern people in her day owned slaves to do their work they had to exercise in some way, and although this might look a little rude to some in these days, but then in the south the young lady most skilled as a horseback rider was thought to be fine. May received from her mother a love for such sport. She became expert as a horseback rider and feared no horse. As the country was new with forests of breezy trees all around, she delighted in riding as fast as she could go. She and Ward would often ride out together, and as he was full of mischief, he would try her skill at running horses. This she could do as well as he, except in standing on the horse's back, which was a feat she could not accomplish, while he could ride in that manner as fast as the horse could go. He was so full of mischief that sometimes when she was not expecting it he would give her horse a cut with the whip, which would cause it to spring from under her and she would alight on the ground. But this she thought nothing of as she was fortunate in never getting hurt. As strange as it now will seem, she often had horses run with her and was often thrown off but never hurt. I saw a horse run with her one time, and every moment I expected her to be killed. There were visiting at her home a gentleman and his wife who came on horseback. They tied their horses at her father's gate and went into the house. May thought now was her chance for a horseback ride. She therefore untied one of the horses and went to a neighbor's house about a half mile from her home to see a sick lady of whom she thought a great deal. When she got there she tied her horse and went into the house. The horses were fine, large, black ones that fairly disdained the ground they walked upon. As the distance was not very far the horse which she tied at her friend's gate could see its mate at her father's gate. This made the animal so impatient that it reared and pitched to get back to the other horse. A gentleman visiting at the house untied the horse and held it until May was ready to go home. He told her she had better be a little careful, but she never thought of fear, and as everybody knew, was a fine rider. He helped her on the horse, but when she got on it reared up in the air and stood on its hind feet. The man, somewhat excited, told May to let the reins loose. This she did, but the fractious horse took the bits in its mouth, and she therefore was as one upon the water in a boat without an oar. The horse dashed away at full speed. As the road was newly made there were stumps of trees on either side. The animal did not keep the road but flew along among those stumps with all its might. May said she expected every moment to land against a tree, as she could no more guide the horse than she could an angry tiger. She had the presence of mind to take her foot out of the stirrup. By this time the horse tied at her father's gate had broken loose and come to meet the other one, with one of the rails of the fence still tied to its bridle, which in its speed swung from one side of the road to the other. Her folks by this time saw her situation and ran to her assistance with all of their might. In passing her brother William's house, little Lulu saw May, and all breathless thought she would do all she could, and ran towards her grandpa's house, but the horse in its speed left the little girl far behind. For once May saw death stare her in the face. To remain on the horse she knew would be almost certain death, so she with one tremendous bound sprang from the horse, and in doing so caught it by the bridle. The other horse was only a few rods away but the gentleman who owned the horses was now by her side. He said, "Hold the horse if you can until I get there." And this May did, for she knew that it was her fault, and if the horses should get away they would go to their home, which was fifteen miles distant. That she well knew would make lots of trouble. Soon little Lulu arrived all out of breath and excited to tell grandma of May's narrow escape. Lulu was very, very much attached to May although so different in disposition. A great many other just such narrow escapes as this, did May pass through, being thrown from horses or having them run with her, and yet for some unseen purpose God in his mercy spared her life. But as "God's ways are not our ways," and "His thoughts are not our thoughts," still in his own good time he doeth all things well.

Ward I do not know as much about as I do of May, although I know he was just as full of mischief and more daring if anything. I remember one time that he and May were playing with

matches, when Mr. and Mrs. Montroville were not
at home. It was many, many years ago, and while
they were very young. They started a fire in the
edge of a little hay marsh for the sport of whipping it out, and then setting it on fire again, just
for the fun of it. Finally there came a gust of
wind that sent the fire beyond their control. This
scared the children, yet the thing was done. The
fire swept along like the speed of lightning. The
little marsh joined a large hay marsh, and the fire
ran for, miles and miles. This reminds me that
no doubt often large fires are kindled and a great
deal of mischief often done through the carelessness of children, who are only at play. Of course
Ward and May were frightened almost to death,
yet they could not help it then. They only
did it for fun, never dreaming of the mischief
it would cause. At another time Ward wished
to take his sister sleigh riding. He happened
to have no sleigh, so he thought he would
arrange one of his own planning. I do not
know just how he arranged it, but I know that he
had no thills to his sleigh. So he hitched the horse
to the sleigh with the tugs of the harness. The
horse he drove was a fast one that ran away every
chance it had. But it made no difference to him.
He was not one of the kind of boys who was
afraid of anything. It was fine sleighing so they
started. They thought they would take one of
the neighbor's girls with them. But the mother

of the little girl did not like the looks of the vehicle and did not let her go. But Ward and May thought it all right, they went up and down hills with such speed that the tugs worked well. When about two miles from home they happened to notice their father, who had been away from home, coming toward them. They knew he would not approve of what they were doing, so in their haste to turn around the tugs did not work well. They of course were not stiff like thills, and the sleigh upset frightening the horse and causing it to run away. Ward and May were thrown out, but Ward was too expert to let the horse get away from him. He held on to the lines, narrowly escaping being struck by a stump of a tree. Finally he succeeded in stopping the horse and they got on the sleigh again. Ward let the horse out, for well he knew that his father would not approve of such work. But before they got home the horse ran away again. And still God in his mercy spared their lives. Many other times did they pass through just such tricks. I remember at one time, when Ward was quite young, his father was away from home and there were some young men at their house. One of them thought, because Ward was little he could do as he pleased with him. He therefore stopped him and threw him on the ground, and hurt him in many ways. Ward stood it as long as he could, but at last forbearance ceased to be a virtue. His southern blood burned in his veins and he sprang for his father's rifle. The young man saw vengeance in his eye, and knew on the impulse of the moment something must be done, and started to run turning the corner of the house, and just as he did so Ward shot, tearing a hole through the house. But as some unseen hand stayed the ball, the young man's life was spared. Of course as soon as it was done Ward was very sorry. The young man knew he was himself to blame and at once made friends with Ward. I only speak of this to show how careful a person should be with a child. When they are young they will in haste do things that they would not do in after life for anything in the world. In just one moment after Ward shot he would not have done it for anything. He loved the young man before, and also afterward. He only did it on the impulse of the moment and would not have killed him for all this world, had it all been gold. No doubt there is many a person to-day wasting life away in prison that acted just as this boy did, on the impulse of a moment. May God in his great mercy stay the hand of any child that attempts to do a wrong thing. He does not always do so. No doubt he did it this time that some good might come out of it.

One day, at Mrs. Bradbury's, we were speaking of the Montroville children: "Well," said Mrs. Bradberry, "did you ever see such children as

5

those Montroville children are? They fairly set
me wild. I do believe they are the worst children I ever saw."

"Well," said Mr. Bradberry, "wife, I don't
know about it. They only give vent to their
nature. They mean all right."

"All right, indeed! I should think they did.
The other day when I was there visiting,"
replied Mrs. Bradberry, "Ward, that mischievous
little rascal, caught a cat and tied a rattlebox to
her tail, and then she went squalling enough to
deafen everybody."

"Ha! ha! ha!" laughed Mr. Bradberry, "That
boy always puts me in mind of Putnam, the General, I mean. You remember the story about him,
when only a boy, climbing the tree after a bird's
nest, and the limb broke quite off, letting him fall,
but not to the ground. His fall was arrested by
one of the lower branches of the tree, which
caught in his pantaloons, and held him suspended
in mid air with his head downward. 'Put, are
you hurt?' cried one of the boys. 'Not hurt,'
answered the undaunted boy, 'but puzzled how to
get down.' At last he cried to a boy equally as
brave as himself, and who afterwards fought
bravely by Gen. Putnam's side, 'Randall, shoot
me down.' Crack, rang the sound of Randall's
rifle and Putnam fell to the ground."

"It is a shame for boys to act so," said Mrs.
Bradberry.

" Well, it does seem so," replied Mr. Bradberry, " but nevertheless none of your sleepy boys for me. A boy ought to run, jump, play, climb, yell."

" Well, then," said Mrs. Bradberry, " Ward Montroville must be a real boy. Why, I saw him climb a great tall tree, just like a squirrel, turn hand-springs, and run a horse as fast as he could go, standing on its back.

CHAPTER VIII.

I do not know but the reader will think me digressing from my subject, yet my intention in writing this story is, if it is possible for me to do so, to bring out the great truth of home influence in the rearing of children. It has been my privilege for a number of years, to be a close observer of the training of children, and my mind has been so terribly pained—oftimes to see bright and intelligent children, who, had they been well educated and trained aright, would have been a great blessing to the world and to humanity, yet on account of their early teaching have often filled drunkard's or pauper's graves, or at least led lives of wickedness. May God in his mercy help us as a people to "raise the blood-stained banner of Prince Emanuel," that we may be missionaries in our own beloved America, to save the rising generation. Of course, in well regulated families the children are protected from many things, but in families that are not so well regulated such is not the case. The mind of a child is easily influenced by those with whom it is brought in contact. I think the first impressions of a child are good and pure. Although we are born naturally sinful, yet, Adam and Eve did not sin until they were tempted; therefore, if temptation had not been in their way they would not have sinned. Although they should have overcome temptation. A child, when surrounded by wicked and bad influences will readily take to those things that it should not. One or two of the most truthful children I ever saw, while very young were surrounded by bad influences. I soon noticed a change in the little ones, who soon became rough, bad, and also untruthful. I think if those children had been raised by good and pure people they would have been the purest of earth's children. Perhaps I can express the idea that I am trying to express better and more plainly by an other figure. You may take a French child, or a child of any other country, and place it in an English family. It makes no difference whether its parents could speak one word of English or not, unless the child is deaf and dumb, it will speak the English language. Just so you may take the child of wicked and uneducated people, and place it with good people, let it be educated and well trained, and nine cases out of ten the child will be like the people who raised it. We often see good christian people who have bad children, for which I think there is always a cause. Some times it is because they indulge their children too much. But if you give it close attention you will surely find some cause.

Eunice Williams, who was taken captive by

savages of Canada one hundred and seventy-five
years ago, was the daughter of a most saintly
minister, of the old Puritan stamp. But a very
few years of savage life made her a savage. Her
mind was cut off from all culture and good society,
and could only tend to savage ways. She retained
a knowledge of her history, and many years after
her capture revisited her home, accompanied by
her dusky husband; but no persuasion could tempt
her to give up her savage life.

"Well," said a friend to whom I was speaking,
"I don't know about the duty of parents to their
children. If they are going to be bad they will be
so any way."

"Perhaps," said I, "my dear friend, you might
just as well say a man might plant a garden, and
never cultivate it at all. He could say if it is going
to be a good garden it will be so, any way; but
will it, if not tended?"

My friend replied, "now there is old preacher
S———'s children. Just look, if you please, at
them. They are the worst children in the whole
neighborhood. They swear, steal and lie. What
can you say about them? You will surely admit
that their father is a good man."

"Yes, indeed I will, but nevertheless he both
neglects and indulges his children too much. You
know the bible says, 'spare the rod and spoil the
child,' but it does not say to use the rod unless it
is necessary. Again it says, 'train up a child in

the way he should go, and when he is old he will not depart from it.' "

" I don't care," said my friend, " I do believe that ministers of the Gospel have just the worst children in the world, now don't you ? "

" No," said I, " I do not. I know we often hear the expression that preachers' children are worse than any other children, but we do not think this is always true. If it were true, I think there would be a very good cause for it. Ministers have to be away from home much of the time. Their children are exposed to all kinds of society. They are humored and petted by many people, and scolded at and despised by others; therefore, I think there are good reasons why ministers' children naturally have many temptations to encounter, and yet I do believe if you will watch them from the cradle to the grave you will find that most of them make good men and women, and that they have to bear a great many cruel and unkind remarks from people who like to slur the ministry. Yet I believe in cause and effect, and the same thing is true of a minister's child, as well as any other."

CHAPTER IX.

May was very young when she began teaching school, and she looked upon it as a fine event in her life, being but a child in years. Possessing a warm and impulsive nature, she won many hearts to her. She did quite well in her school, although had she in her early years been taught the necessity of obedience, and the noble traits that go to make a success in life, how much better she might have done.

We will here describe May. She was about medium size; with black eyes and hair, and a dark complexion. Her hair she wore in heavy braids that hung far below her waist. She was only seventeen, possessing a very romantic nature, and had always been indulged in having her own way. She soon formed many new acquaintances. Life began to have many new charms for her. She enjoyed the many new changes.

As I had formed quite an attachment to May, and felt very much interested in her welfare, I thought I would visit her at her school. It was noon when I arrived and I found May alone in the school house, while the children were at play in the yard.

" Oh, how delighted I am to see you," said May.

"I thought perhaps ˹you would be lonesome, away as you are among strangers, so I thought I would come and see you."

"Oh, I am very glad you came, but I am not one bit lonesome. I am having just splendid times."

"I am glad to know you are happy and enjoying yourself. But May you are young, and away among strangers, you must be a little careful how you conduct yourself."

"Oh," said May, "do not worry one bit about me, I am very capable of taking care of myself. You know I am a teacher, and of course I am capable of doing as I please."

"Well, how are you getting along with your school?"

"Quite well, but I don't care quite as much about teaching as I thought I should; but I am just perfectly enchanted with the young people around here, they are just fine. Oh! I tell you I am having grand times."

I could plainly see in May's dark eyes, that there was some great attraction among the young people. "Well May," said I, "you are young and away from home, now you must remember, 'All is not gold that glitters.'"

"Pshaw!" said May, "you are always preaching a sermon. I know I can take care of myself. I am sure a girl seventeen years old is just as able to care for herself as she ever will be."

" I know they should be ; yet some girls are more capable at ten than some at your age."

" Well, I don't care, I am having fine times and I hope you will not say one word to mar my happiness. Oh, dear me ! " continued May, " I do wish you could know how much fun I have. I am just perfectly happy. Tell mother not to worry one bit about me, for I will get along alright."

No wonder she was happy, for it was beautiful scenery that surrounded her on every side. The school house was situated in just the right place for one of her nature to enjoy. To the right and rear of it, almost up to the windows was a fine forest of beautiful trees, and it being just the beginning of spring, all nature seemed grand. My heart was almost overcome by the grandeur of nature. The wild bird warbled its thrilling notes amid the lofty trees, and flitted with joyful melody on either side. In front of the school house broad fields stretched far westward and before her school closed they were covered with golden grain that waved on the summer breeze. Everything looked so grand that her heart constantly beat with wild admiration. She had not been teaching long before she formed the acquaintance of a young man to whom she soon became much attached. He was most elegant in form, with handsome, sparkling eyes, and teeth of pearly whiteness, just her ideal of manly beauty. He being much older than she and more experienced in the ways of the

world, did all in his power to win the heart of
May. We will call him William Bryant. They
spent hours together, either at her boarding place
or taking walks picking wild flowers, or in sitting
in shady groves. He looked upon her as almost a
child in years. But still his heart went out in
love and admiration for her wild and dauntless
though childlike ways. She had not known much
of life's sorrows; all then was joy and happiness.
The earth, to her, seemed almost a heaven. As
she spent hours listening to his words of love or
as she slipped her hand in his, he would breathe
words of tenderest love into her ear.

He was constantly by her side. He could not
bear to have any of the other young men, who
would gladly have taken his place in May's affections, share her company. He seemed constantly to feast upon her society and the days
passed happily away. I will here mention one
walk they took. He called at her boarding place
one beautiful Sunday afternoon and asked her to
take a walk with him. After wandering about
for some time, and becoming considerably tired,
they sat down under the shade of a tree. The sun
was just setting, and threw its rays of light
around them. The sky was clear above and the
soft breezes played among the leaves in the trees
over their heads. Every thing seemed grand and
sublime and threw a magic spell around them.
Their hearts were filled with joy and happiness.

A sweet silence seemed to reign as if an angel hovered about them. Earth, just now, had no sorrow for them, for earth's sweetest love filled their hearts. Happy indeed was May as Mr. Bryant took her hand in his and looking with tender love into her eyes, asked her to become his wife. Too happy to answer him just then, because of the love that filled her breast, yet she became his betrothed. They sat for some time enjoying the silence that reigned, and then softly wandered back to May's boarding place, little dreaming of the sorrow they were going to pass through in after life.

The summer passed away, bearing much pleasure and happiness with it. Finally the last day of school came, as all things have to come to an end, and these days too happy to last, at last were ended. The parting was very tender. Hard indeed it was for May to leave the place where she had enjoyed herself so much. One mistake no doubt which May made was on account of her age. She set the time of her marriage in the far away future. Perhaps if they had then been married all would have ended well, but May was young and looked forward to accomplish much with her education. She wanted to enjoy young society and did not care to become a married woman so young. This I think was alright, but I doubt the propriety of so young a girl being allowed to place her affections on a young man.

Mothers do wrong in permitting their girls to accept of steady company so young.

After she closed her school she returned home, but there was an aching void. A sadness filled her heart. Although glad to see her friends again yet her home did not seem as it did in days of yore. Her mother tried to make things pleasant, but her heart constantly sighed for other scenes and for friends far away. She was naturally proud and knew full well that her folks were poor. This she felt all the more keenly from the fact that early in life her father had been quite wealthy, having everything at that time to make life pleasant. But it was not so since his reverse in fortune. This hurt and pained her so much that she felt she could not have her lover, the one on whom her entire happiness depended, come to see her, for his people were well off, and possessed everything to make life pleasant. She knew that it would make a difference with them. She knew that he had a vain, proud-hearted mother who desired that her son should marry for wealth and position. This she keenly felt, and although as much as she loved him, she felt she could not have him come to see her. She loved her own folks and felt very sorry for them, for she knew it was no fault of theirs that they were now so poor. Yet she felt that it would almost kill her for him to know of her poverty. She also felt that wealth and influence have a great deal to do in securing friends in this sinful world. Weeks rolled into months and still she did not see him, only hearing from him through the mail. Her heart constantly sighed for him, and she longed to once more be folded in his arms and to listen to his words of tender love. Tears would blind her eyes as she thought of happy days gone by.

After months had passed, unexpectedly he came to see her. She met him and naturally as might have been expected was very much pleased at seeing him again, although she was very much embarrassed at his becoming acquainted with the fact her family were poor. If at this time she had been able to ask the assistance of the One that can heal all sorrows, the One that gave His life a ransom for the sins of this wicked world, and had looked to Him, she could have been better able to have borne the sorrow of this embarrassment. But she could not say Thy will be done, for she did not know at this time how to thus be comforted. After making his visit, he bade her farewell, and returned to his home. She went to her room and wept bitterly. She thought this visit might be the last one that she would ever enjoy with him. Yet she knew he loved her more than any one else, but she thought that his friends desired him to marry some wealthy lady. Being proud and ambitious, this pained her very much. After his return home she received several letters from him, but once or twice she heard, through communications from

other friends, that he was paying attention to
another lady, one of wealth, and one who suited
his mother very much. Yet in his heart he could
not forget the girl he truly loved better than all
else in this world. But being rather sickly, and
influenced by his friends, he gradually crushed the
memory of the one he loved. Months rolled by,
and still he spent much time with the lady of
wealth, and no doubt forming some attachment
for her. Kindly he wrote to May that his health
was very poor, that he would never marry, and for
her to write him a farewell letter. This pierced
her heart through and through. She tried often
to write him a letter and tell him that her heart
was breaking, that she could not give him up, but
the tears would blind her eyes and she could not
write. Her grief was almost more than she could
bear. At times her proud nature would assert
itself, and she would think : " If this is all he cares
for me I will give him up," but it was easier thus
to think than it was to do. There came over her
mind a sad and melancholy gloom, which she
could not shake off. The world to her had lost all
of its sweetness. So very young, yet her heart
had lost all its joy. Nothing but sadness filled her
mind. None of the joy of youth filled her heart.
She was gradually wasting her life away. She
tried sometimes to rally, and again enjoy youth
and happiness, but this she could not do. The
world seemed to have lost all of its happiness.

Ah! then she remembered that the world at large sought the bible for comfort and peace. She then began to read this holy book, to see if she could find comfort there, and as strange as it may seem, she found no comfort there. This was because she read it as she would have read any other book. She did not read it with the spirit of understanding, nor a faith that will not shrink, though pressed by every foe. After reading the blessed bible, one or two chapters every day, for over one year, and still remaining sad and despondent, receiving no comfort from it, there began to hover around her mind a darkness that almost caused her ruin for time and eternity. She began to gradually lose all faith in the bible, and the things that truly go to make a happy life. She leaned entirely upon her own weakness to gain strength. If she had said within herself, " Here Lord, I give myself to thee, it is all that I can do," then would she have gained strength. But this she did not do. She did not understand how to gain strength and comfort from reading the Holy bible. She therefore began to disbelieve its teachings. She did not receive the peace that it spoke of. All was darkness. Her soul was overwhelmed with grief. Months had passed by. Ofttimes she had attempted to write the farewell letter, but just as often, amid blinding tears, and with a grief stricken heart, did she fail to express to him (the one she loved far better than her own life) the grief that was crushing her heart, and causing the sorrow of life to be more than she was able to bear, and making the awful abyss of hell to stare her in the face. At last she gave up the idea of writing. She thought he should never know the sorrow she felt (which he never did) and that she would try and give him up. It was not long after this that he married the lady of wealth. When May heard of this the noble nature within her rallied. She said to me, " he now is the husband of another, and it is not right for me to mourn for a married man."

" No, indeed," said I, " let him go."

She therefore took his picture, the last thing she had to remind her of him; took a last, half frightened look at it, and then cast it in the fire and burned it up. Her nature was too noble to mourn for a married man. She therefore began to forget the one great sorrow of her life; but still her nature was changed. Such sorrows leave their impress on our natures. Her heart was hardened. She seemed to care nothing for the things of life. The words of the Gospel fell on her ear, " As sounding brass, or a tinkling cymbal." But all the time she tried to let no one know of her sorrow. She did not want to let any one know that she doubted the doctrine of the bible, but as for herself she could not feel the peace that it spoke of. Life, nature, the bible, all had lost their charms.

She now came to me for comfort, but my advice

6

seemed to do but little good. So changed was she, yet so quietly did she bear her grief, that her most intimate friends knew not of the sorrow she felt, or the pain she was passing through. But as time rolled on, she knew that she must try and make the best of life. Others sought her hand in marriage, but she could not make up her mind to ever again think of placing her affections on any one. The sorrow of the past was too severe to think of again trusting any one that might cause her sorrow. After the marriage of her old lover, she heard but little of him. The distance between them was a number of miles, and she tried in every way to forget him. Shè felt that she never again wanted to see or hear from him. One great advantage to her was that no one in the neighborhood where she lived knew of her former engagement. Therefore they knew nothing about the mortification she felt at being treated so by one who should have treated her differently.

Many were the scenes she constantly passed through, but the worst of all was that she seemed to have no feeling in regard to religion. How dark and sad life is, when trouble and disappointment overshadows our mind and soul, and when all of earth's miseries crush us to the extent of our being, and no one to go to for help. To try to struggle with life's tempestuous tide, leaning only on our own strength. Had she leaned upon her Saviour and listened to his gentle voice, she would have received strength. But this she did not do. She tried sometimes to forget all of the past, but found it very difficult to do. Past sorrows and disappointments are not as easily forgotten as one might think, and for her it was almost impossible. Being of so nervous a temperament this sorrow seemed greater than she was able to bear, and especially trying to bear it as she did, in her own strength.

CHAPTER X.

As we have already said, Mrs. Montroville was a healthy woman, who took the household cares upon herself, not depending upon May for much assistance. Now comes a change, and one that throws much care and responsibility on May. Mrs. Montroville is taken suddenly very ill with a malignant fever. Anxiety now fills the mind of every member of her family, and it is feared that she may not recover. Her sons stand by her bedside, and try to soothe her pain. Mr. Montroville, seeing that death is drawing near, does all in his power to have the dreadful monster stayed. May's bleeding heart knows not what to do, for she had leaned so heavily upon her mother. Now as she stands by her bedside and holds her feeble hands in her own, she fears that her mother will soon be gone.

" Well," said I to May, " death is pronounced upon all of the sons and daughters of Adam. We must look upon it only as a visitation to be expected by all mankind, the high as well as the low."

Mrs. Montroville had made a great pet of her little granddaughter Lulu, as Lulu's mother had always cast the care of the child upon her. She now felt great anxiety for Lulu. She knew that May was old enough to take care of herself, but in her wild delirium, she constantly spoke of Lulu, often exclaiming: "But she is little. She is little." She feared that when she was gone the little darling might be neglected. Little Lulu would not leave her grandmother's house. She remained both night and day, that she might be near her dear grandma. At last the hour was drawing near. Early in the morning of a winter's day, Mrs. Montroville called her friends to her side. She said she could not stay long, and asked that Lulu might sit by her on the bed. She looked upon her little, helpless form, and the only favor she asked of Mr. Montroville was that he would always take care of little Lulu, which he solemnly promised to do. She lingered unconsciously until the middle of the afternoon, then closed her eyes forever to the things of earth, to bask in an eternity of sunshine, in a world that is free from care.

May now was surrounded with sorrow on every side, but she had some warm friends and also some bitter enemies on account of a hasty temper which was the result of nervousness and entirely beyond her control. Those of her friends who were true now came forward and showed themselves such. Among the number was a young man who had become an intimate friend of May's, who did all he could to comfort her, and while friends were paying their last tribute of respect to her mother, this

young man, whom we will call young LaMarr,
stood by May's side and tried to help her bear her
grief. Of course as a friend in time of need she
could not help appreciating his kindness.

After the funeral, Oh! how sad to return to that
lonely home! May, who had never known much
of household care, now had to take the place of
her mother. It was nearly night when we arrived
home. The very things that were around her
mother, May and I had to put away. Everything
was so dark and dismal. Oh! now how much she
needed the grace of God to help her in her lonely
lot. But this she did not have. Mr. Montroville's
health was fast failing, which made it much worse
for May, as he was not much company for her.

As I could not stay long at Mr. Montroville's, it
would have been almost impossible for May to
have kept house for her father had it not been for
little Lulu. William and his wife were willing to
have her live with May, who just idolized the
child. They were constantly together. May had
no company with whom Lulu was not a welcome
guest. May used what means she had to dress
Lulu and as she was very pretty, she felt proud of
her little curly-headed niece. Lulu was very
active and had a great desire to help with the
work. She seemed to want a part to do, and
usually in the morning, as the work was being
done, would take a small basin and cloth and go
out into the yard and wash the pump, as if it was

quite necessary that the pump should be washed every morning just the same as the dishes. May thought everything Lulu did was very cute. Although May was very quick tempered, yet with Lulu she was always kind. Mr. Montroville, too, was very fond of Lulu.

Now that his father's health seemed gradually failing him, William and his wife usually spent their evenings with him. William loved to talk of his days while in the army, and never seemed to lose sight of the changing scenes of war. He always referred to it with pride. No coward's blood ran in his veins. He was one of those noble boys who was willing to brave the battle field, and if necessary to have lain down his life for those he loved. William was a great comfort to May's lonely lot. He was more cheerful than any of the rest of the family. May sadly missed her mother. It is very lonely for a girl to keep house without her mother. I noticed although hasty and impulsive as May was, and imprudent too, yet through a great many sorrows and afflictions, the dear Savior watched over her, and although she felt not his love and tender care, yet in an unseen way he was gently leading her. His sympathy was toward her for the blind way she sought or tried to seek comfort from the holy bible, and gained none. She thought then she had done all in her power to gain the assistance of divine help, if there was such a thing to be gained. And

because she received not forgiveness for her
sins, her way was so dark that finally she almost
gave up in despair, and although she loved
the truth, and everything that goes to make a
noble life, yet with regard to religion she was en-
entirely in the dark. But as God's ways are not
our ways, yet in an unknown way to her, he was
leading her, and although she did not then know or
feel his mercy, in his own way he was bringing
her to understand that the things of life were
nothing to compare with his mercy and truth. Of
course the things he has given us to enjoy are good
in their places, but as her's was a selfish nature
she thought too much of the things of this life.
She had such a love for those things that are of the
world, that the dear Savior had to lead her through
many places in bringing her to the true light of
the Gospel, that made her heart sick and sore, and
over ways that left her feet pierced and bleeding.
Oh! the darkness of earth that hung around her
soul! She did not feel the love and comfort that
the blessed Savior of the world has promised to
those that ask in faith believing. James: 1 chap.,
6 verse.

I will mention here that it is best to associate
with christian people, although we do not feel
their love, or that our hearts will gradually unite to
theirs. No doubt if this girl had always been with
wicked and sinful people she might have always
remained in the dark, and her soul would have

been eternally lost. Oh, how much better it is in the morning of life to give the heart to God; and commit all of our ways to Him. Then we will omit many of the sins and lusts of youth that will be thrown around our pathway; for just as we sow, we shall reap. How grand and sublime it is for children to " Remember their Creator in the days of their youth," before the cares and sorrows of life come upon them, for then they will have a strong hand to lean upon; and an eye that never sleeps to watch over their ways and to direct their path; for as sure as they do they have the promise " commit thy ways to the Lord and he will direct thy path." What a grand promise, and as sure as God is true this will be so. The whole mistake in regard to the Gospel is; in not believing, and in not submitting our souls into the hands of God. Of course this is easy enough to those who do believe, but to those who are in the dark it is not so easy, for "the devil goeth about like a roaring lion seeking whom he may devour," and as he is very cunning he weaves his web around the heart of the unbeliever, and holds him in his grasp. It is hard for some people to understand these mysteries, and they remain in the dark until some extraordinary thing brings them into the glorious light of the Gospel. All are not constituted alike. What will do for one does not always do for another. " God's ways are not our ways," but all his paths are peace. Bless his holy name.

"But May," said I, "you must ask in faith, nothing wavering, for he that wavereth is like the waves of the sea, driven with the winds and tossed. You are as one drifting on the ocean of time, drifting you know not where."

Although young yet May had a great deal of experience in the things of the world. The hand of death had made its inroad into her family. But as she knew more of suffering now than she did earlier in life, she tried to bear it as bravely as she could. Several friends within a short time had died who had lived christian lives. This of course left the greatest impression on her mind of anything in regard to religion, as it always does. The holy, upright life of the christian is the greatest thing in the world to bring the unbelieving heart to God. At the time of the death of her mother there came to her a different feeling.

I noticed a change, "What is it?" said I to May.

"Well," said May, "it seems as if something was helping me to bear the sorrow."

At one time she said there came to her an unearthly feeling as if an angel or a heavenly light shown around her, and although it affected her, and she often wondered what it could be, yet her heart and mind was so in the dark that she almost disbelieved the power of God, and that death would be the end of all earthly things. No doubt ofttimes amid the sorrows she encountered, the blessed Savior gladly would have shared them with her, if she had only believed on his holy name. But that she thought was impossible for her to do. Ofttimes she thought if there was such a thing as prayer that she would pray, but her prayers were as her belief, without faith.

"If we receive," said I, "we must ask in faith, believing, then we shall receive. But we must ask not for things to consume upon our lusts for then," said I, "our desires may be of a selfish nature and the blessed Savior may not grant our petitions, for as an earthly parent pittieth his children, so also doth our heavenly father pity them that love an serve him. And a great many times we may ask for things that would not be well for us to have. This the One that knoweth all things, knows, therefore He does not always grant everything we ask for, because He knows it might cause us trouble, and in many ways it would not be well for us, and because He loves us He with-holds them. But we have this promise, that no good thing will He withhold (that is, nothing that would be good for us to have). But we are com-manded to pray, we must pray. But let us humbly ask that we may pray aright, for oft times we get into the dark by asking for things that would not be well for us to have, therefore we do not always receive."

CHAPTER XI.

"I called to day to see William Montroville," said Mr. Bradberry, " he is very sick."

Mrs. Bradberry replied, "I am very sorry indeed. What do you think is the matter with him ?"

" Well, he caught cold and now has lung fever."

" I suppose they have a doctor by this time ?"

" Yes, they employed Dr. D——."

" Well, what did the doctor say ?"

" He said it would be a very doubtful case. You see William has no care whatever. His wife acts more as if he were a brute than a human being. Poor boy, his has been a hard lot."

" Yes, indeed it has. I don't suppose he ever had one decent meal of victuals in his own house, unless someone besides his wife got it for him. No wonder the poor boy is sick, such indigestible food is enough to make any one sick."

" Well," said Mr. Bradberry, " The doctor said to me, he never before saw such a woman in his whole life. Why, he said she fairly abuses William."

" I guess we had better go over and see him as soon as possible."

" Yes, indeed we must," said Mrs. Bradberry.

The same afternoon Mrs. Bradberry and I went

to see how William was getting along. I was surprised to see how very sick he was. He was lying on his back, his face was tinged with a yellowish hue, his eyes were rolled away back in his head. In an instant his wife came into the room where he was.

"Your husband is very sick, is he not?" said Mrs. Bradberry.

"Oh!" said his wife, "he is always a great hand to make a fuss when anything is the matter with him."

"Surely he is very sick and something should be done at once," said Mrs. Bradberry.

"Well, if anybody wants anything done they will have to do it themselves. I have done all I intend to do. I don't care if he would die; then perhaps I could have a little comfort."

At this unfeeling remark, Mrs. Bradberry, in perfect astonishment said, "Why, you must not talk so."

Not long after we had been in the house the doctor arrived. He stepped to the bed, looked at William, felt of his pulse, and then pushed back his sleeves, as if bound to do all he could. You could plainly see a troubled look on his face.

"I will give ten dollars, out of my own pocket, to have Dr. W——, of T——, brought here for counsel, as quick as possible. This young man must live, and I have done everything in my power."

The doctor he referred to was one of the oldest as well as one of the best in the whole country, but lived at a town some twelve or fifteen miles away.

Then turning to Mrs. Bradberry he said, " Montroville is very, very sick, but he must live." He then turned and looked at the baby and pointing at it said, " What would become of that little one? Yes, he must live. This is a difficult case, everything is so uncomfortable, but nevertheless for the sake of those children I am bound to do all in my power. He must live, yes he must live." After a moment's thought he said, "As I have a very fast horse, I will go myself." Then turning to me he said, " You stay here until I return. Be sure and keep him well covered up as he is liable to take cold. I will return just as quick as possible."

I watched the doctor as he drove away. He jumped into his cutter, wrapped his robe around him, and then dashed away at great speed.

" Why," said William's wife, "what a fuss that doctor always makes. I felt like ordering him out of the house. I suppose he thinks me not capable of tending to my own house; but I shall show him about it. He better not come back here again showing his authority, or he will get his walking papers. Lulu, you good-for-nothing thing, sit down or I will give you a slap," said she.

Not long after the doctor went away William

awoke and began to talk. " Do you feel better ? "
said I.

" No," was the reply, " I do not." He then
turned around and as May was standing by her
brother's bedside he said to her, " May, come here."

" What will you have ?" said she.

" Well May," said he, taking her hand in his, " I
am going to die."

" Oh! my dear brother," said May, as she kneeled
by his side, "do not say that. We cannot give
you up."

" But, May, poor May, it is so. I cannot long
remain here. I have nothing to live for but my
children. You know how very unpleasantly I am
situated. May, I made a sad mistake when I was
only a young boy. I married when I was only, as
you might say, a child. This marriage has blighted
my life. But by it there have come to me
children. Poor, dear, darling little children.
Oh! May, I now have to leave them in a cold
and sinful world. I have not much to leave
them ; and May, you know Jane is not capable of
taking care of them. Oh! May, dear May, when
I am gone, will you be kind to them? I know it
will be hard for you, but May it is hard for a poor
little orphan child to live among strangers. There
is my poor little curly headed Lulu, sweet little
girl that she is, please look after her. Dear little
Charley I will give to Ward. I know he has
children of his own, but I know he will do all he

can for him. He has a good wife. But my baby Willie, poor little baby boy. I expect Jane will have to keep him." Here his feelings overcame him and he broke down and wept. "Oh! may God in his great mercy take care of the little fellow. Oh, I fear, I fear for him. Oh! May, dear May, if I could write with my heart's blood, I would warn the young to be careful about that great and most important step of choosing a life companion. But then, it is often hard to tell. You know that Jane seemed all right at first. But May, when I am gone be kind to my children, my dear little orphan babes."

"Yes brother, dear brother, I will do all I can for them," said May, as she knelt by his bed, her face flooded with tears.

I then went to his wife and asked her if she believed him dying, but little did she seem to care. She only cared for herself. William, tortured with pain, sometimes rolled in wild delirium on his bed. May stood by him and smoothed his auburn hair. It happened that there was an entertainment at the school house near by. Almost the entire neighborhood were there, both young and old. Of course May would have been glad to go, as she enjoyed such things very much, yet she knew she was more needed by her brother. William becoming somewhat better, looked into her face and said, "You will not leave me all alone." This touched May's heart. "No," she said, "I would not leave my darling brother all alone for all of the entertainments in the world." She would rather stand by the bedside of her brother and try to ease his pain.

Mrs. Bradberry had returned home and the doctor had not yet arrived. Myself, the wife, and sister, were now alone. The shades of night had gathered and a loneliness hovered around. William at last expressed a desire to sit up and be dressed. May told him it would not do for him to get up, as he might take cold. After this he lay quietly in a very straight position, talking some. The wife retired in another room for the night. A neighbor came in to stay with May, and help take care of William. After a little while he seemed to rest well. May watched the clock, and just at eight she prepared his medicine. As she stepped to the bedside she beheld the pallor of death spreading its mantle over her brother's face. Her friend stepped to the bedside and they together beheld him gently breathe his last. He fell asleep in death as softly as a little babe goes to sleep upon its mother's breast. They stood for a moment horror struck. May felt she could not stand by the death bed any longer, and said to her friend, "Stay here while I go for assistance." She sprang to the door and out into the darkness. She was very much excited, her only thought being to get her brother Ward there, and as God has promised to always be with those in trouble so in this

8

case he afforded assistance to May. She had gone but a short distance when she overtook a cutter with a young lady and gentleman out sleigh riding. They took her in the cutter. The young man drove as fast as he could to the school house. May rushed into the school house and up to her brother Ward and said, "Come, William is dying." Ward bounded like a wild deer to the door, and soon stood by the bedside of his dear brother. May's friends tried to quiet her, and told her that she was only excited, that William was better. But she knew that she was not mistaken, but that he was dead, as they were all soon made to realize. This was a sad hour. All was excitement. A young man folded in the arms of death unexpectedly. It threw a sadness over all.

Mr. Montroville, who was at home, knew nothing of the death of his son. He was shortly afterward summoned to the bedside, and he came in great haste, thinking perhaps his son might want to see him. But as he came in and saw that death had done its work, and as he looked upon the pale face of his son, he wrung his hands with grief. His heart was crushed. His oldest son, his darling boy, the one whose assistance he most needed, gone, forever gone.

"Dear, oh dear!" said Mrs. Bradberry, "what will become of those poor little children ?"

"Sure enough," said her husband, "poor little ones." Mr. Bradberry sat with his hands upon his head for some time, and then said, "If I were able I would take all of those little children. Poor little Lulu is such a frail child. What will become of them is more than I can tell. If their mother were only capable of taking care of them."

"Well," said Mrs. Bradberry, "you know she is not, therefore it is a very difficult case. Yes, indeed, for anybody that takes those children will always have trouble with that woman, of course they will. She acts as if she naturally despised everybody and everything. But nevertheless those dear little children should not suffer on account of their mother. I must confess I am puzzled to know what will become of them, they are all so very young. Can we do anything?"

We have now come to the place in our story where we are compelled to describe the wife of William. Although it is a painful task for me to do, causing my brain to reel and my blood to run cold, yet truth is truth, showing no injustice to any one. Glad indeed, would I be if I could describe her in any other way than the way I will have to. She was one of those silly, trifling women, who had no love for her husband nor her home, although she had influenced William to marry her when he was only a little past seventeen, she being much older than he. At first he seemed very much attached to her, but as he learned the ways of the world and saw how slovenly and good-for-nothing she was, and how she tried in every way to make him unhappy, his love for her apparently wore away. She belonged to one of earth's noble and good families, having one of the best and purest hearted brothers I ever knew, who tried to do everything in his power to make her a better woman, and cause her to care more for her children and her home. Yet for all he could do she was the same trifling, careless woman. May God in his great mercy protect the children of such a mother. I do not think ever in the records of time was there a more helpless little orphan family than this one. This woman not only neglected her children, but seemed to despise those who tried to take care of the little darling ones. I have often been made to weep, when I thought of William, a bright and noble young man, who was brought to sorrow and no doubt the grave, by a trifling woman. While they kept house few were the comforts he enjoyed. The house was always nasty and dirty, with nothing pleasant, although he was very neat.

CHAPTER XII.

The friends of William soon gathered at his house, and to the astonishment of all they found that May's message was true, and that he was dead. Friends rendered all the sympathy and assistance that they could to this bleeding-hearted family. Yet this sorrow, time could never change, or at least could not restore the dear one back to life again. Mr. Montroville was crushed and overwhelmed with grief at the loss of his son, and as his health was so poor he could scarcely stand the sorrow and excitement, it was thought best that Ward should take his father back to his house to stay with him, and see if he could not be more reconciled and get some rest. But the sorrow was too great. No doubt he thought of William's helpless little orphan children. He knew his own health was gone, and that William's wife was worse than no woman at all. Well indeed would it have been for this family and for those little children had they been motherless also, for their mother was entirely incapable of taking care of them, both on account of her careless and willful nature, and because she possessed no faculty for taking care of children. Mr. Montroville was agonized with pain and sorrow all night. He could not rest.   The grief he bore was too great to afford the peaceful sleep that comes to the tired body.   When the mind is over burdened, as the troubled sea, it cannot rest.   At dawn of day he arose, and as the sun mounted the heavens, shedding light and beauty all around, he stood by his chamber window that looked over the fields to William's residence, where his son's lifeless body lay.

He said to Ward, " It is a beautiful morning, but it affords no happiness to me."

Although a christian, yet there are times in a christian's life when the barge is so tempest tossed that this earth can not give peace; that heaven alone can give the rest our weary souls thirst for.

Ward had to attend to making the arrangements for the funeral.   May, although all worn out, yet remained at the home of her brother to help care for the children and get things ready for the last sad rites over one she had loved so well in life. At last the hour arrived, and the lifeless body was borne from the sad home, amid the blinding tears of a grief stricken family.   There was a large congregation of sympathizing friends, who filled the school house where the funeral services were held. As little Charlie wept and cried for his father there was hardly a person who did not shed tears.

Mr. Montroville, as he was taking the last look at his son, in the language of King David exclaimed,

"Oh! my son, would to God I had died for thee my son, Oh! my son!"

After the body had been laid to rest in the quiet grave, and they had returned home, a good christian minister accompanied Mr. Montroville home, to try and afford some sympathy. But the stroke had been too great. His feeble frame gave away and "the brittle thread of life was almost severed." He sank into a decline, would have no doctor, would take no medicine, and once or twice while great drops of sweat (although his body was icy cold) trickled down his cheeks, he said to May and a young friend of hers who stood by his bedside, " you know nothing of the pain I am now experiencing." Yet he bore it so peacefully, although nervous and impatient; but now as the sands of life had nearly ceased to run, so mild and patient did he wait, and as the minister asked him his hopes of heaven, he trustingly replied : " with the rest of mankind I must stand my chance." A short time after this, about the same hour of the night, just one week from the day that William died, he spoke to Ward (Ward and May were now alone with their father as the minister had just gone away) and said that he would like to get up, as he was tired of lying on the bed. Ward assisted him to arise, and as he was supporting his father in his arms, his life gave away. Ward noticed the change and called May to his side. They together laid the trembling form of their father on the

bed. He tried to look once more into their face,
and then the lamp of life ceased to burn. Friends
were soon summoned to their assistance. Kind indeed were those warm-hearted people who rendered love and sympathy now to Ward and May·
No doubt their hearts would have been crushed
had it not been for the kind and loving acts of
friends who tried to afford them all the comfort
they could. Noble indeed is the person who will
try in time of sorrow to help a friend bear a grief,
and to smooth the rugged paths of life. Ofttimes
when the heart is sore and bleeding, just one little
word or sometimes a tender look help make the
tide of life flow much more peacefully. Just one
week from the very hour, in the little old fashioned
school house the funeral dirge again was sung; but
now the family had dwindled down until the
mourners were few. Ward and May now occupied
the same seat that their father did just one week
before, but now by him it would be forever vacant.

Ward took the death of his father very hard.
He now felt himself almost alone. He well knew
how much depended upon him. He had been so
much attached to his father and brother, of both of
whom he had been bereft in one short week.
May seemed more resigned yet she felt the help-
lessness of William's little children. After the
burial they returned to their lonely home, for the
death of Mr. Montroville left May entirely alone
in her father's house. Ward thought best that she

should stay at his house until other arrangements could be made. As I have said before, little Charlie also lived with Ward. Dear little Lulu now lived with her mother in that sad and dismal home.

In a little while after this Ward took possession of his father's farm and moved in his house. As he was the only one capable of attending to the farm and settling the estate, this duty he performed in a good and honorable manner. May still remained with him. Things were now so changed, in so short a time, but they all did as well as they could to make the best out of life. Had it not been for William's family they could have got along very well, but on account of the inability of his widow to take care of her children, as well as herself, it made things very unpleasant. Ward had all of the responsibility resting upon him that any one person ought to have, yet he was willing to do all he could for his brother's family. May's love for Lulu was intense, but as she was now situated it was impossible for her to do as much for the child as she would have been glad to have done. It was not long after the death of her father, that Lulu was taken very sick. Again May was called to stand by a bed of suffering. Her heart was very much pained for the little one. I will here describe one very severe trial she had to encounter. There was a woman who lived near, a woman who had been a grass widow of Irish descent, who came into the neighborhood an entire stranger, and by some method succeeded in influencing a well-to-do farmer to marry her. This of course elevated her very much. But as her heart was as hard as stone, and as the work of the evil one is always shrewd and cunning, so this wicked woman, whom we will call Rebecca, which was her true name, hastened to this house. She was accompanied by another woman and also by her brother. They found May, Lulu, and her mother alone. Lulu was very sick. She marched in with the dignity of a queen, but her heart was as wicked as the evil one could have wanted it to have been. She took in the situation at a glance, and well knew that Lulu's mother was not capable of taking care of her. She also knew that she could sow discord and make trouble between May and the mother. So she began in the most abusive language she could command, saying that Lulu was not being well taken care of. She seemed to direct all of her abuse upon May and the other members of May's family who were not present. She chided and insulted in every way that her vile tongue was capable of. She claimed to have done much for them, but in fact had done very little, which no doubt in her eyes looked very large. May stood her abuse as long as it was possible for one of her hasty temper. At last her fiery southern blood arose. She told the woman she had better mind her own business, hinting that she perhaps did not know what people thought of her. At this the woman's brother began on May. He, too, possessed much of the overbearing disposition of his sister. Now May became so enraged that she said many things she ought not to have said, forgetting in the excitement of the moment all about little darling Lulu. For a while pandemonium seemed to reign. The woman's vile tongue seemed fired with a viper's sting. All at once May happened to look at little Lulu, whose little innocent eyes were bent on her. This was enough for May, who read the look of love on Lulu's lonely face. Lulu looked to May for her care. Although a little child, yet she had long ago learned where her care came from. May was overcome at once. She well knew there was need of good and speedy care for Lulu. After the woman left May was all excitement. Death had made such a sad inroad into her family that she felt they could not spare dear, precious little Lulu.

Oh! if Lulu's mother could only have been capable of taking care of her, but as this was impossible it was a very trying position for May. She was young and had never taken care of a sick child, therefore she felt her inability to take care of her now that she was so very sick, and yet to act, seeing Lulu's mother was present was very hard. It was almost dark. May knew something must be done, she therefore went to see if she could hire a good old Quaker lady to come and take care of Lulu, a lady who understood medicine and was a good nurse. As it happened I was at the lady's house when May came. I saw she was very much excited as well as very much grieved about Lulu. She at once made her business known. She seemed to have no time to lose.

"I came," said she, "to see if I could get you to go and help take care of Lulu, as she is very sick and we know not what to do."

"Did thee not know my boy was sick?"

"Of course I did not, or I should not of come," said May.

"I feel very sorry for thee, but I can not leave my child, to take care of thy niece."

"Well," said May, "I do not wish you to do so, but we are in trouble. Lulu is very sick, and I am afraid that if we do not get something done at once dear little Lulu will die."

"Thee go back and do what thee can, and she may get better," said the lady.

"But folks are accusing us of neglecting dear, darling Lulu," said May.

"Who is accusing thee of neglecting her?" the good lady asked.

"Mrs. Rebecca F—— came to-day with some of her friends, and she abused us in the most insulting way, saying that it was only put on, that we only made believe that we cared for Lulu. She also threw out slurs against my friends who have just been laid in the grave. Oh, dear, what shall I do?"

" Well, replied the good Quaker lady, " we all know what kind of a woman she is. Her tongue is ever ready to condemn the innocent. But never mind. May, go back, do the best thee can and God will bless thee." Then turning to me she said, " it is a shame for Rebecca to so abuse May. Had it not been for the Montroville's taking her in when a stranger and protecting her, Edmund would never have married her, but now I suppose she feels independent. As the bible says, ' cast not thy pearls before swine, least they turn again and rend thee,' I suppose this is the way she is paying them back."

" Well," said I, " I do feel very sorry for the Montroville's. They are having a very hard time. We all know and so does this Rebecca, that Lulu's mother is not capable of taking care of the children when they are well, much less when they are sick. Yet she is very hard to get along with. She is not willing for the Montroville's to do as they would like to by the children. Of course this wicked woman knew this, so she has been trying to make trouble. But the devil always wants some one to do his work and always uses just such persons as she to perform it."

Then turning to May, I said, " I will go home with you and do all I can."

But as my experience was about as little as was May's, I felt incapable of doing as much good as I should have been glad to have done.

" As we started, I noticed that May was all excitement, she rushed along almost on the run, and exclaimed, " Oh, I do not know what to do for dear Lulu! I can not give her up, she is my only comfort. Dear, dear Lulu, the little darling girl. I would rather die than to give her up. Tears streamed down May's face. Although quick tempered, yet May's heart was very tender.

"Well, May," said I, "we will do the best we can. There yet may be some chance for Lulu to get better." But I noticed May was very anxious to get back to Lulu, though she did not say very much. It had become very dark, the roads were muddy, and as we hastened along we saw a light at the lonely dwelling, and as we approached the house we heard voices and soon discovered that there were people in the house talking to Lulu and her mother. As we entered the house we soon noticed that there were several neighbors, also a gentleman and lady, people of culture and refinement, who had come in while May was gone. May had become so nervous and excited that she could not understand who the people were. Turning to me she inquired, in a whisper, "who are those people? Are they friends or are they foes?" But this I could not tell, as I had never before seen them.

The gentleman observed that we were somewhat astonished at their being there, so turning to me he said, "I was very much surprised a few days ago to hear that my dear friend, William

Montroville, was dead." He continued, saying that he knew William very well while in the army. " William was one of my bravest and best soldiers," said he. " I have never seen a man who was more daring on the battle field. He feared not the cannon's roar, and when blood run fast and deep we could always depend on him. I learned to love him for his warm and noble spirit. Although loyal, yet he possessed much of the warm nature of southern people, and because of this he was of great service to us. A few days ago I learned the sad news of his death. I felt very much pained that I did not learn of it in time to attend the funeral, and now I have come to see if I can be of any service to his family."

We soon were made to understand who the gentleman was. He was an officer in the regiment that William belonged to while in the army, and hearing of William's death, and no doubt learning of the situation of his family, had come, bringing with him his noble wife, to assist in taking care of William's children. I noticed he was very much surprised in William's wife. He at once observed, as might any intelligent person, that she was unfitted to take care of the children. He watched May for a while, and then remarked to me, " I see the look of William in his sister. I know she must be his sister," said he, as she is almost his very picture."

" Yes," said I, " May is his only sister. She was

very much attached to her brothers, and now seems to possess an undying love for his children, especially little Lulu."

"The little girl is very sick, is she not?" said he. "There must be something done for her at once!"

At this May came up and said, "Yes, dear little Lulu is very sick. I do wish something could be done for her. We have lost so many friends that we cannot give Lulu up."

At this the officer's face first grew red, then turned pale. "Yes," said he, "there must be something done. My wife is a splendid nurse. She will be glad to take care of the little girl for a while until other assistance can be provided."

At this May was so glad she did not know hardly what to do. Now instead of pandemonium, Elysian shades seemed to have gathered.

"How I pity those little children of William Montroville's," said Mrs. Bradberry, "because it is no small job to properly care for little children. The impressions made on the mind of a child are very important indeed,"

"I know they are," said a friend to whom she was talking, "yet we often see little ragged children, fat, and as healthy as they can be. Open air and exercise are just what they need. I well remember, and to my sorrow, too, an accident that happened to me when I was quite a small child. There was a lady visiting at our house who had a

very sweet little baby girl. I played with her and
thought I never before saw a child quite as lovable
as it was. I happened to notice that it had very long
finger nails. I never could tell what caused me to
do it, but nevertheless I took the scissors and cut
the baby's nails, never once thinking of any harm
in so doing. But when it's mother noticed what I
had done the poor woman took her baby and appeared half frightened to death. 'Why,' said she,
' it is a sure sign that a baby will not live one year
if its finger nails are cut before it is a year old.' It
seems that there is an old superstitious saying to
this effect but of course I had never heard it, for
if I had I would not have done it for anything in
the world. I was very much frightened and very
sorry indeed for what I had done. My mother also
gave me a good scolding, which of course I needed.
The poor woman went home believing that her
child would surely die, and as strange as it may
seem, the baby did not live more than two weeks.
But of course the cutting of those nails had no
more to do with its death, than do any of those
old superstitious sayings. But when my poor
mother heard it she thoughtlessly gave me another very severe scolding, never once thinking of
the injury she was doing me. Of course I thought
I had surely caused that sweet little babe's death.
I naturally was very nervous, and that baby's
death so frightened me that I truly believe I suffered every pang of an actual criminal. After I

8

had retired to bed I would begin to think of the
baby, would turn icy cold and tremble from head
to foot. I would sometimes imagine that I could
hear demons in my room. I began to feel very
poorly in health, and finally went into a nervous
decline. I did not speak to my mother about the
cause of my suffering, because I was afraid to do
so. Poor woman, kind and good as she was to me,
yet they had made the wrong impression on my
mind, which neither they nor any medical skill
could cure. For months and months I suffered
and suffered, and even after years had rolled away
I would turn icy cold when I thought of that sweet
little baby, and as strange as it may seem, I never
fully recovered until I was old enough to learn for
myself how foolish such superstitious sayings were.
In reality I had only done what should have been
done by its mother, for with its long nails it naturally would hurt its poor little self. I always
feel very indignant at those willful nurses that
will frighten little children half to death in order
to make them afraid of them."

"Yes," said Mrs. Bradberry's friend, "I know
there are very many little children that on account of wrong impressions suffer very much, aside
from careless neglect. 'Oh, precious childhood.'
There is naught so sweet as an innocent child. No
wonder the Savior said, 'suffer little children to
come unto me, and forbid them not, for of such is
the kingdom of heaven.' The mind of a child to

thoroughly develop, should be occupied with pleasant amusement, and as it grows older should be encouraged with higher and holier aspirations. I don't believe that a child unless surrounded with things that are bright and cheerful, can possibly be happy."

CHAPTER XIII.

The next morning I thought I would call on Mrs. Rebecca ———, as she lived just across the road, and find out if I could, why she had so abused May. I therefore went.

"Good morning, Mrs. ———, nice morning."

"Very nice. Come in and be seated."

"Your folks all seem to be well and enjoying the blessings of life and a pleasant home."

"Oh! yes, we usually are well, and have much to enjoy in our home."

"What a blessing good health and a pleasant home is. But all people are not so fortunate as to have them."

"I suppose there are some who are not, but usually, I think, it is their own fault."

"Well," said I, "I hear the Montrovilles are having a sad time now that little Lulu is sick."

"Oh! they are always having a bad time. Some folks make a great fuss over a mighty little thing."

"Yes, but sickness, and death, are not such little things, after all," said I. "Have you been over to see them?"

"Yes, but I'll not step my foot in the house again, if they all lay there and die," said she.

"What is your reason for saying so?"

" Oh ! yesterday I called there, with my brother and a friend, and I just happened to remark that the Montrovilles always pretended to think so much of Lulu, but that it was no such a thing, as the child was really suffering for care. May sat there all dressed in mourning, as if she had lost every friend in the world," said Rebecca.

" Well, you know she has in a short time lost mother, father, and brother, and has not many relatives left. No doubt she feels like dressing in mourning."

" Well, as I was saying, I just made Jane—by this she meant Lulu's mother, although it was not her true name, but by this name we now will call her—understand about what I thought. I just said everything I could think of. I got fighting mad. I told May she had better take off that dress and do something for Lulu."

" Well," said I, " but you know there is Lulu's mother who does not like May very much, which makes it hard for her to do anything. It is a pity that Jane cannot take care of her children."

" Oh ! yes, but she don't know enough to come in out of the rain," Rebecca replied, " and if she did, she is so trifling and dirty that it would make a well person sick for her to do anything for them."

" So you see it is difficult, do you not? The Montrovilles are placed in a very trying position," said I.

" Oh yes, but I would do something," said she.

" Well, what would you do?"

" Well, I would do something!"

" But what would you do?"

" I do not know just what I would do, but I would do something," she went on to say.

" That is just as I thought. It is pretty hard to say just what one will do until they have tried it," said I.

" I don't care. I just gave that good-for-nothing May to understand what I thought of the Montrovilles. At this May got mad and called me all kinds of names. At last my brother took it up, and he told her what he thought of her. We had the young lady just where we wanted her. We give it to her. Jane came very near ordering her out of the house. I told Jane I would, if I were her. At this May stamped her foot and said it was her father's house, and then she ordered my brother out of doors."

" Well, it is her father's house, or was when he was living, and I suppose she thought she had a perfect right to order him out."

" But I want you to understand that he did not go. He just got up and I thought he would strike her, for she is one of the most provoking things I ever saw. He was just giving her fits, when lo, and behold, in came one of her gentleman friends, and don't you believe he had the impudence to pull off his coat as quick as a flash, and step up to my brother and demand what all this fuss was about. At this my brother said not another word, but just left the house at once, as he always thinks peace is the best thing. That fellow no doubt thinks himself very brave. My brother is twice as large as he is. But you know he did not believe in quarreling, because he loves peace."

"No doubt," said I, "in that case it was best for him to love peace, because that fellow, although not as large as your brother, is not to be fooled with."

"But didn't I tell him as soon as my brother was gone that no one was to blame but May?" Rebecca replied.

"What did he say then?" said I.

"Oh! he said he did not wish to quarrel with a woman."

"Well, I expect he is somewhat as I am, does not want to see it all on one side of a question."

"Well, I don't care, my brother and I both felt like stomping May, and I believe he would have done it, if that impudent fellow had not come just as he did."

At this she became so excited, and talked so loud, that her husband came in to see what was going on. I now thought I had better say no more to her on the subject, so I said "Good morning, Mr. F———."

"Good morning," said he, "we are having some excitement this morning"—winking at me as if to say, he was not quite well pleased with the way his wife was going on.

"Oh, your wife and I were just talking about those Montrovilles. I suppose you know they are again afflicted?"

"Yes. Poor little Lulu is such a nice little girl, I am very sorry for her. It is a pity that her mother is such a careless person."

"What do you think about them?" said I.

"Well, I must confess, that I do not know what to think. I never before saw such a difficult case. It is very sad on account of the inability of Lulu's mother to take care of her children." Then Mr· F——— went on to say that he had known Jane since she was a little girl and that she was always just so trifling. No one could ever do anything with her.

"Oh yes," said I, "I think I have heard that you are a distant relative of Jane."

"Yes," replied Mr. F———, "I am. Jane and I were raised together. I lived in the same family with her for years. Her father was one of the nicest men I ever knew. He was a man who was loved and respected by all who knew him."

"It is very strange, then," said I, "that Jane is the person she is, so incapable of taking care of her children."

"Well," said Mr. F———, "Jane, while yet very young, was afflicted with a very peculiar disease, which affected her mentally. Although at first it was not noticed much, yet I think that it grows on her. Her father spent hundreds of dollars on her, but it was of no use, although since she has grown to be a woman she enjoys good health. Yet she possesses no faculty of making her home pleasant or doing any kind of work well."

"It made it very bad for William, he married her while he was yet very young and upon very short acquaintance."

" Her mother told me that if she had had any idea of their getting married she would have told William all about Jane. But she said that never such an idea entered her head. Jane knew that her folks were opposed to her getting married, she therefore was married unbeknown to them. Of course we kept it quite secret about her inability to learn to work. In this I now think we did wrong. In some respects Jane was quick and active, and while young looked very well, but as the care of a family became hers to perform she seemed to lose all ability to do anything as it should be done. My first wife, who now lies in her grave said that she never felt so sorry for any one in her life as she did for Mr. Montroville, William's father. Shortly after William married Jane, Mr. Montroville knew that I was a distant relative of hers, and after William had brought his wife home to live with his folks, Mr. Montroville at once noticed that she was no wife for William. He therefore came to our house to inquire about her. Of course my dear wife could not lie and just told him the truth. It fairly overcome Mr. Montroville who at once saw that his boy was ruined, and we felt very sorry for him. Mr. Montroville was a very intelligent man, who loved his children very much. He was also a very nice man and one who did not believe in people being divorced after marriage. 'Now that they are married,' said he, 'we will have to make the best of it. It was for Mr. Montroville's sake I have ever felt a great interest in William and his children."

"What a pity," said I, "that a young boy should have made such a mistake and brought such sorrow on his friends; but he was young and no doubt loved well, but not wisely, and as she belonged to a nice family I suppose he thought he was doing well."

"Well," said Mr. F——, "I know some people lay great stress upon the character of the family that a person marries into, but I think wisdom should dictate the choice, and not the family. Some of the worst marriages I ever knew, were those of people who belonged to good families. Of course it is a good thing, if possible, to belong to a good family, but the family is not all. Some of the best and greatest persons who ever lived were those belonging to ordinary families."

Said I, "this marriage has taught me that you are right, that people in chosing a companion had

better look at the person, instead of trying to find
out whether their ancestors were born of noble
blood, or cradled in a manger."

" I know," said Mr. F———, "there are some
low people who censure the Montrovilles, but I
guess I know as well as anyone that they are not
to blame. I was very much opposed to my wife's
conduct in abusing them yesterday."

At this a clear voice rang out from the kitchen :
" You had better mind your own business; you
will stick up for those low-lived Montrovilles;
that is all you know. You think that those children, especially Lulu, are little angels, but I want
you to understand that you, or no one else, in my
house shall so applaud that trifling set." At this
Mrs. Rebecca came rushing in, and in the most
abusive language told Mr. F——— what she
thought of him. Her tongue, I thought, came the
nearest to perpetual motion of anything yet discovered.

At this Mr. F——— replied, " If I were you and
made the profession of religion that you do, I
would not talk so about the Montrovilles. Did
they not when you were a stranger, take you in
and do all they could for you ? If it had not been
for them I never should have married you."

" Oh ! married me ! I did not marry you ! It
was your money I married. But now, thanks to
myself, I do not need their sympathy, or yours

either; one third of your money is enough to make me independent."

" Oh yes! I have long since learned that it was my money and not me you married," getting excited and stamping his foot upon the floor, he exclaimed. " Yes, because of my dear wife, my first love, the wife of my bosom, who now lies in the grave, I do love those Montrovilles. Yes, and for her sake I love that hot-headed May, too, and William's little orphan children." Then turning to me he said, " My dear wife was much attached to the Montrovilles, before her death. She and May spent hours together. She loved May and dear little Lulu, and if I did not know that they had been kind to this woman that now so abuses them, I might think differently."

I now saw that both were getting so excited that I had better go, so I therefore bade them good bye and departed."   .

As I was leaving this home of comfort, possessing many of the luxuries of life, I could but think how little this woman appreciated its comforts. My mind wandered to the book of Ecclesiastes, to the words of King Solomon, 5 chap., 10 v., " He that loveth silver shall not be satisfied with silver; nor he that loveth abundance with increase."

As I entered the dismal dwelling where the suffering child lay, I could but notice the difference in the two homes. This one being so untidy, everything dirty and uncomfortable. I said in my heart, oh, earth! thy ways are hard to understand, but then I rejoice in that blessed promise, " That the rough places should be made smooth." While I was gone the gentleman and lady had taken their departure, promising to return before long. Now Jane, Lulu, and myself were alone, so I thought I would try and get on the good side of Jane, as I knew this was quite important for Lulu's sake.

" Well, Jane,". said I, "I think that Mrs. F—— was very much out of place yesterday in talking as she did, and in trying to make hard feelings between you and the Montrovilles."

" Well," said Jane, " maybe she was, but then I don't like to have May here trying to take care of Lulu. I guess she thinks I don't know enough to take care of my own children. I just want her to stay away and mind her own business and I will take care of myself."

" But," said I, " you know Lulu is very near to May, for Lulu has always lived with May, and her parents."

At this little Lulu said, " ma, why do you not want Aunt May to stay with us? She is so good to me. I want aunt May right by me."

I now noticed how much better Lulu was, after the good care she had received from the good lady and her husband, who had so kindly taken care of her all through the long hours of the night.

Lulu was a very thoughtful child. She very

well understood her mother's inability to take care
of her. She had always been taken care of by her
grandma, until her death, and since that time May
had looked after her with a mother's tender love.
I never saw a mother watch her child with more
tender care than did May watch Lulu. I have
often remarked that the love that should have
burned in her mother's breast, God for some
reason unknown, planted in the heart of May.
Although May and Lulu, as I have said before,
were just as different as they could be. May was
very quick tempered, nervous, and impatient,
while Lulu was mild, gentle, and lovable, a gem
of purity and innocence. I now said to Jane as
gently as I could, " oh! well, you had better be
willing for May to help you take care of Lulu, as
Lulu wants her so badly."

At this Jane said, " no, I do not want the good-
for-nothing thing to come here again."

At this Lulu began to cry and said, " oh! ma, I
do want Aunt May to take care of me, for if she
don't I will die."

I now quickly changed the conversation. I saw
it would not do for Lulu to hear any more, so I
laughingly said, " never mind, Lulu, we will take
good care of you ; and just as soon as you are able
I will take you to town and get you something
nice." This seemed to satisfy the child, and she
now dropped to sleep.

Just then I happened to look out of the window,

and who should I see but the gentleman and lady again drive up. They got out of their sleigh and came into the house.

" We were so interested about the little girl," said the lady that we could not be content at home, and have come back to see if we could not render farther service."

" I have been thinking, said the gentleman, that as my business calls for my constant attention at home, as also does my wife's, that if all are agreed, we will take the little child to our home and do all in our power for her. Just then in came the doctor, and as Lulu was still sleeping the gentleman made his intentions known to him. The doctor seemed very much pleased, as well as surprised to meet so fine a gentleman and lady there.

" By all means," said the doctor, " to stay is death, to go may be a chance for life. The little girl seems to be a very fine child; takes after her father. I was well acquainted with him. He was a noble fellow."

The doctor then awoke Lulu, and pronounced her some better. He asked her if she would not like to take a sleigh ride, and get away from her unpleasant home. Lulu seemed delighted. They then consulted Lulu's mother, and she seemed glad to have her go.

" The gentleman, his wife, and the doctor held a private conversation, which they seemed not to want us to hear, after which the gentleman said, "wife and I will go home and make necessary arrangements, and return as soon as possible."

The gentleman's home was not many miles away, and with his fine horses they soon made the trip. They returned, bringing with them, nicely arranged in their sleigh, a nice warm bed, with soft woolen blankets, and everything to make the little girl comfortable. And then as lovingly as a tender mother she bore the little girl away to their comfortable home. It seemed almost like rescuing the little girl from the jaws of death. She was so well cared for that the ride appeared to do her good. The gentleman had no children of his own, although he had a father's heart. The lady was one of those angelic, motherly women, who took the little girl in her fond embrace and did all in her power to restore her to health again. They stood by the little child all night, watching almost every change of breath, so anxious were they for the morning to dawn to see if the ride had made the child worse. But at the break of day, the little girl awoke, looked around to see where she was, and as the lady bent over her she recognized her friend and began to smile. The lady now saw that the child was much better. They now took new courage to labor on.

CHAPTER XIV.

This noble gentleman, and lady, now opened their hearts, as well as their home to May and Lulu's mother. The lady remarked to me, " Lulu is very sick. I fear she may never be any better, and while at my house her friends are welcome to see her as often as they wish."

Days passed by and still the little girl remained very low, sometimes it was thought she could not possibly live through the long hours of the night, but still this kind lady and gentleman stood by the little sufferer and watched her with a parent's tender care. At one time, in the dead hour of the night, it seemed that the little girl's breath was growing shorter, the little frail form lay so help- less. The lady stood by her as long as she could and then left the room.

"I found my wife weeping bitterly," remarked the gentleman. "I said to her, cheer up we will not give the little girl up. She will live for some good purpose yet, I hope."

As they returned to the bedside where the child lay, hardly knowing whether the gem or just the casket would remain, to their delight the breath came faster, the flush of the rose tinted the pale cheek of the child and hope still remained. How animated they together labored on, and with the the aid of the skillful physician, the child began to recover. May now seemed very much delighted, and said to me, "dear little Lulu will now recover, but I fear if she goes back to her home with the care she will there receive, she may again be sick. Oh, dear! if she could only live with this lady she would be so well taken care of."

Lulu made rapid progress toward recovery, and just as May had feared, as soon as the child was able to sit up, her mother began to urge her to go home; and of course, child like, Lulu thought it would be nice to again be at home. Jane would coax and tease the child when alone until she would cry and tease the lady to take her home. Of course the lady knew that no doubt by carelessness the child would be exposed to all kinds of weather and again be sick. Yet ladylike she said it is her mother, and I do not wish to dictate, yet I do fear for the child. When May found out how things were going, she told Lulu that she had better stay with the kind lady, " for," said she, " if you go home you may take cold and then you will be sick again and no doubt die."

As Lulu was a very thoughtful child she knew what May had said was true, she therefore said no more about going home until she had fully recovered. The lady said to me, "I never saw such influence as May exerts over Lulu. After her mother had coaxed her to come home I could scarcely take care of the child. Of course," said she, "Lulu is young and knows not what is best for her, but she has good judgment; much more than her mother."

"Yes," said I, "I do wish some good person could take the child and raise her as she should be raised, for she is a lovely girl."

"Yes, indeed," said the lady, "Lulu is a very fine little girl, but it would be very hard for any one to get along with her mother. The child would be a thousand times better off if she had no mother. Then some one could take the child and care for her, but the way it is, it would be impossible to do anything with her, as her mother uses no reason or judgment."

Jane went home to stay, but as it was lonesome there she thought it would be just as well for Lulu at home as it was for her, so back she went to the gentleman's house after Lulu. Finally, after nothing else would do, they took Lulu home, no doubt regretting that the little girl was not their own.

Much might be said in praise of this gentleman and lady. Their work was a work well done. It has been many years since that gentleman heard the welcome summons: "Well done thou good and faithful servant, enter thou into thy rest," and as "the memory of the just is blessed," he still lives to-day in my memory, and as "a good name is rather to be chosen than great riches," what name is above the name of one who will deny self

for the love they have for suffering humanity?
The lady still lives, and still her work, noble indeed, is for the good of orphan children.

Jane now undertook to keep house, but wretched
work indeed did she make of it. Things were so
illy arranged and so untidy, that there was not one
ray of cheerfulness there. Sad is the home where
the mother has no faculty of making things cheerful. This one thing does more toward wayward
and wandering children than anything else.
Wealth is not necessarily required to make home
pleasant. It is well to study the likes and dislikes
of children. Little things in a child's life are
those that are long remembered. The child is
quick to notice any defect in its parent or its
home. My heart has often been pained by careless, trifling parents, who have been the means of
bringing bright and intelligent children into the
world, and then act as if their mission was done,
and let them grow up just like weeds, without ex-
erting themselves for their welfare, and often com-
plaining, "Oh! my family is so large I can
scarcely provide bread for them to eat." "I have
no time or money with which to educate my children." Who is to blame, I would ask, for the
large family? The child or the parent? Oan a
child help being brought into the world by a low,
trifling parent? I answer, no, no more than the
child born to a king can help being the child of
royal blood. Yet ofttimes the innocent child that

is born to a low parent, not only suffers by having to be raised in a dismal and sickly home, but is pointed out by children that happen to be born to parents of higher and nobler blood as the child of Old So and So. Many are the hearts of poor little children that have bled, on account of just such treatment; that have felt the world's cold frown, and well understood the cause. But it was beyond their power to help their condition.

I feel to reproach the parent who by low passions will bring helpless children into the world, and then do nothing to make home pleasant for them. A father who has no tender love for his offspring is not fit for a father. Parents who are not capable of raising their children right, should not have children. I think it is a mistake for persons who are authorized to marry people to solemnize a marriage where the applicants are not persons capable of bringing up children as they should be brought up. I am glad that the law now of the United States compels parents to send their children a short time each year to school. Yet, sorry that the law is not enforced as it should be.

It is always such low persons, as I have tried to describe, should one of their children struggle through all the discouragements as well as embarrassments, and make a success in life, who dwell on the commandment, " Honor thy father and thy mother," forgetting that the first duty is from the parent to the child, instead of the child to the parent. "Parents provoke not your children to wrath, but bring them up in the fear and admonition of the Lord."

I knew a father once who had a very intelligent son. The son was ambitious, and bound to make a success of life. He labored hard to accumulate some property. The old man became so indignant at his son because he would not spend all of his money to uphold him in business, and procure him drink that he applied to the county for assistance in order to disgrace him.

As Lulu was getting old enough to look a little after her own welfare, she did not, as had been anticipated, have a relapse, but there was little to make her cheerful and happy. Little Willie, (the baby) of whom we have before spoken as a bright little fellow, was just as cute as he could be. He would try and amuse himself in every imaginable way. He had a great idea of being a doctor, and very often would do up paper in little packages, similar to those done up by doctors for their powders, and then feel of our pulses and say, " you are sick, you had better take some medicine." Then he would give some of his little powders to us. I have often thought had he been well taken care of he might have made a very smart man, but the little fellow was allowed to run around in the cold, ofttimes barefooted; not for the want of shoes, but because his mother was too indolent to put them on, or had no idea of the importance of keeping her children warm and properly dressed in uncomfortable weather. It was one cold day in March. Snow still remained on the ground. The little fellow had been playing in the snow barefooted, which of course he could not endure, and he was too young to know what was best for himself. I called, with a friend to see how the children were getting along, and Jane told us that Willie had a chill. I was not at all surprised, as I knew how he had been exposed to the weather. I said to the child, "Willie, you are sick, are you not?" He made no reply. I noticed he had some fever, and apparently was quite sick.

"Well," said I to Jane, "we will go down to Ward's and take dinner, and after dinner we will return to see how Willie is getting along."

The reason we went to Ward's for our dinner was because Jane never tried to entertain any one, and if she did at any time muster up enough energy to get a meal of victuals, it was in such a condition that a person of any intelligence could not partake of it. As we were going to Wards', who lived just a short distance from Jane's, my friend remarked to me, "it is just awful how those little children have to be exposed to all kinds of bad management. How strange it is that they are such nice and intelligent children."

"Did you ever before see such a difficult case to manage?" said I.

"No, indeed I did not. No wonder William died so young. He had the hardest time to enjoy life of any one I ever knew. Jane is so indolent, and as far as I can see, of no earthly account to any one."

While at the table eating dinner we were startled by piercing screams. On rushing to the door we beheld Lulu, running as fast as she could toward Ward's house, crying and calling for May to the extent of her voice. Ward and May fairly flew to Jane's house, knowing something must be the matter, and truly enough there little Willie lay in hard spasms. We did all we could for the little sufferer. Ward mounted a horse, and went at full speed for the doctor, but ere the doctor arrived, death had come to the little child's relief.

On enquiring of Jane the cause of the sudden change in Willie, she said that Rebecca F——, the woman May had so much trouble with, came over and brought some medicine to give Willie.

" Did you give it to him," said I ? "

" Yes," said Jane.

" How much did you give him ? "

" Oh ! I gave him a spoonful."

" I fear you gave him too much."

" Well, I gave it to him, and whether too much or too little, it was given, and there is no use in crying over spilt milk."

" But I fear you gave him too much. Did not Rebecca tell you how much to give ? "

"I don't know whether she did or not," said Jane.

On learning about the medicine we found out that it was very powerful, and should only be given to adults in drops: " I am very sorry that Rebecca would handle medicine so carelessly," said I.

"I suppose," said Jane, " you think me not capable of doctoring my own children. I want you to understand that I will do for my children just as I please, and it's nobody's business."

" Yes," said I, " but you must be careful how you give medicine, you know it is not to be fooled with."

"Well," said Jane, " it is nobody's business what I give or what I do for my children. I shall after this do just as I please. I was bossed around by one man, and I do not intend that anybody else shall say what I shall or shall not do.

" Well," said the doctor, who had arrived, " you had better not give your children any more of that medicine, or any other medicine unless you know better how to handle it than you now do."

" I shall do just as I please about my children, and people may say or think just what they please," was the reply.

The doctor's quick wit, plainly saw that she was both willful as well as ignorant; then turning to me he said, " it is a pity for such women as she to be mothers of children. I often see cases similar to this where people are raising children, who are no more capable of such an important duty than are the wild Orang outang. Yet it is hard to tell in such cases what it is best to do. Is not this little girl, referring to Lulu, a lovely child?"

"We all did what we could to save her while at Mr. M——'s, but it now looks like a poor chance for the child. When her grandparents were alive she was well taken care of, but now things are very different."

The doctor examined the body of little Willie, but he knew it would do no good to state the exact cause of his death, as the poor little fellow was much better off than to live in that dismal home, and also because the medicine had been given through carelessness, instead of any intention on the part of its mother to harm the child. Although a good many thought that it was the medicine that killed the child, I never felt satisfied as to the true cause of its death.

After the funeral Jane made up her mind that she would take Lulu and go to a town a few miles away, and live with a sister of hers. She therefore made arrangements to go. The night before she started she and Lulu stayed at Ward's. Of course all felt bad to have Lulu go. May said to me, "oh! how can I stand it to have dear little Lulu go?"

"Well May," said I, "as you have no home for her it may be best for her to go."

"Oh yes," said May. But I could see that it was almost killing her to have the dear little girl go, but as she had no home to offer the child she could do nothing but submit.

During the evening, Young La Marr came in to spend the last night with May and Lulu. He was very much attached to the child, and as he always in time of trouble tried to befriend May, he now knew this would be an awful trial to May to see little Lulu go away. But May tried to make the best of it. She said, "dear Lulu, you will be a good little girl, for you have always been one. It may be best for you to go."

"Oh! Aunt May," said Lulu, "you have always been so good to me, how can I stand it without seeing you?"

"Well, Lulu, it is not very far, so I can come to see you sometimes."

"Oh! do come Aunt May, it will be so lonesome without you or Charlie. Oh, if grandma was alive, then I could stay with you."

"Yes," said May, "but, dear Lulu, things are quite different since mother died."

I could read in May's looks that she felt very bad to have Lulu go, so I thought I would try and persuade Jane to be very careful with Lulu. So I said, "now Jane, you will be good to Lulu, as she has been very sick, and if you are not very careful with her she may get sick again."

"I shall do," said Jane, "as I please with my children. I will give them just what I please, and Rebecca will back me for she told me so. After this I am going to show people that I shall do just as I please. I want old W——, she referred to the gentleman who had taken care of Lulu through her sickness, to understand that I did not thank him for h s services. I suppose people think me not able to take care of myself."

I well understood her, so I said, " well Jane, I am glad you feel so capable of doing well by yourself. I do hope you will look well to Lulu's welfare. You know she is a very frail child. What do you intend to do at your sisters?"

"I shall do as I please at my sisters. She always tried to boss me but she will now find out that I am my own boss."

I saw there was no use in talking to her, so I said, " Well do, for mercy sake, be careful of Lulu."

Then May said to me, "dear, oh dear! I cannot endure it to have Lulu dragged around as she will be. I know the dear little girl cannot stand it."

" Well May, you will have to endure it. You see Jane is the child's mother, and as long as she persists in keeping her she can do so; and another thing, you have no home to take the child to. You know that your brother has Charlie, already, also children of his own, besides you make your home with him, therefore you see that there is no other way to do but for Lulu to go."

With tears streaming from her eyes May took

the little girl by the hand and said, " well, Lulu dear, I guess you had better go. I know it is very hard for you, Lulu, yet no doubt it is for the best."

" Oh! Aunt May, I want to stay with you and Charlie."

We all went to see them take the cars. The parting of Lulu and May was very effecting, but I tried to cheer May up as we were returning.

" It is not very far to where Jane is going," said I, " and you can go and see Lulu before long, can you not?"

" No one can tell what she will do with Lulu," replied May. " She may go as did little Willie, or something worse may happen to the child. No one knows the trouble our folks have had in trying to raise those children."

" I know you all have had a very hard time, but you know, ' the darkest hour is just before day.' "

" Oh, dear me! there is no day that can dawn upon that woman's careless ways."

" It does seem as if your statement is almost true, May, for I do believe there is not one person on earth who can do anything with Jane."

The first we heard from Jane was that she had sent Lulu to live with a brother of hers, who resided in the far west, hundred of miles away. May was not at home when the news came, I therefore felt anxious to know how dear little Lulu stood it to be taken hundreds of miles away from the home of her childhood, to see no more the faces of the friends she loved so much. I happened to meet a person who was on the train on which Lulu went away.

"How did the child seem to stand it to be taken so far away?"

"Oh," said the person, " it was just awful. When we came near the station where the Montroville's live, the poor little girl just cried, and cried, and begged to stop and see Charlie and May once more. I do believe every person on the train felt sorry for the child."

"How did her mother stand it?"

"Well," said the person, " she is a strange mother. She hardly shed one tear. She told the little girl to never mind, that she would be better off when she got at her uncle's house. She did not seem to understand that it was very hard for a little child to be sent hundreds of miles away, per-haps never more to see her friends."

"Lulu's mother did not send her all that distance alone, did she?"

"No, she sent her with two women who were going west. I did not like the appearance of the women at all. They seemed perfectly brutal. They told the child there was no use of crying, and tried to make the little girl sit up, as the little girl sat with her head in her lap, weeping as if her heart would break."

"Oh! may the God of heaven protect the dear little girl! How many just such helpless little orphan children there are, who have to be sent to and fro, and feel the world's cold frown."

I afterward learned by another person, that Lulu's uncle met her at the depot in the far away western city to which she was sent. He was a kind gentleman who had always tried to make something out of his sister, but had long ago learned that it was of no use. Therefore he welcomed her little orphan girl. His wife was a noble, intelligent lady, who received Lulu with a warm heart. Yet their ways were different from those to which the child had been accustomed, and though she tried to be happy, yet her little heart was very sad. Night after night, for weeks and even months, her little pillow was wet with tears. Nevertheless the little girl was much better off than with her mother.

We now leave Lulu in the west.

CHAPTER XV.

When May learned that Lulu had been sent so far away she shed many bitter tears, but said, " I know my precious little Lulu will be better off, although it is very hard to think of her hundreds of miles away. I know her uncle is a gentleman, and her aunt is a lady. They will be kind to her, yet the poor little girl will be very lonely without Charlie, or dear little Willie."

"I am glad you look so wisely upon it, May. I was afraid it would almost kill you." I thought I would try and cheer her up so that she would be more reconciled to it, so I said, " Lulu's uncle has a little baby boy, that will be some comfort to her."

" Yes," said May, " no doubt it will, but it is hard for a little child to be so far away from home."

I then thought I would try and make a good impression on her mind. " Well, May," said I, " I know you have seen much of life's sorrow, but why do you not seek comfort from the fount that all true comfort comes from, where you can drink and thirst no more? from the balm that can heal all of earth's sorrows? You oft have read that precious promise, ' Come unto me all ye that labor,

and are heavy laden and I will give you rest.'"
But to this I could get no reply. Within herself
she was a study. She seemed to have no feeling
in regard to religion. I have very often thought
had May listened to the still small voice of her
Savior her pathway would have been much more
free from the thorny way she had to tread. Her
nature was so impulsive, her disposition so fiery,
that she had to be tried in the furnace to take
away the dross.

After the death of her friends she still continued
to teach school in the neighborhood where her
home was. But she was so lonely that she made
up her mind that she would change her employ-
ment and go from the place where she had known
so much of sorrow and disappointment. She
therefore went to a town some miles from her
home and began the business of dress-making.
Here she formed many pleasant acquaintances.
Life began to have new charms. Her heart longed
for friends. Possessing as she did so warm a nature,
she could not bear to be without warm friends.
She always sought if possible to board with a
widow lady that she might have some one to share
her loneliness. She was blessed in this direction,
as several times she boarded with noble, widow
ladies, who did all they could to make it pleasant
for her. I will mention here two of them, both of
whom were lovely christian ladies. Their homes
were very pleasant to her. She loved to listen to

their kind christian advice. She attended church with them, and loved the society of christians best, as she early had been taught to respect christianity and had early learned to honor the holy sanctuary. But her own heart was so cold she was as one living in a world without a God. She had no faith and said she could not believe. She was so in the dark, she could not, or did not try to exert any faith. But as strange as it may seem, she would not for the world say anything against religion. She loved its quiet, cultured way. She loved the sound of the church bell. She loved the songs they sang. She loved the Sabbath school. But to feel the love of Christ in her soul she did not. She knew her own heart was sad, but she did not understand how to break her stubborn will.

Not long after Lulu went away I met May at a friend's house where she was visiting. She had just received several letters, and among the rest was one written in a strange hand. On opening the letter we found it was from dear little Lulu. The little girl was too young, or at least had not yet learned to write, so she had printed as best she could a letter to May, as follows:

DEAR AUNT MAY. I AM WELL I HOPE YOU ARE THE SAME I SAW THE GREAT MISSIPPI RIVER AND MANY OTHER NICE SIGHTS AS I CAME WEST. I WISH YOU COULD BE WITH ME. MY UNCLE AND AUNT ARE GOOD TO ME WELL I MUST CLOSE GOOD, BY LULU.

We all wept over this little letter. The dear little girl was very careful not to say anything that would make May feel worse about being so far from home. She well knew that May could hardly stand it to have her so far from home.

" Well," said May, " I am so glad that Lulu is allowed to write to me, for although the poor little child cannot write yet, those little printed letters are worth more than gold to me."

" Lulu," said I, "is a bright little girl. She makes sunshine wherever she is."

"Oh! yes," said May, "if we who love her so well could only have her. Why are things so strangely arranged?"

" Well, May, I cannot tell. Yet all things are right for those who serve God."

"I cannot understand why we should have so much sorrow. Death is hard to be reconciled to, but there are things that are worse than death. I have stood by the bedside and seen my mother, father and brother die, but it was not half so hard as it is to see William's dear little children taken hundreds of miles away from home. I know dear little Lulu cries herself almost to death. I expect her uncle and aunt are good to her, but just think of the dear little girl, seeing no more the scenes of her childhood; no more to join with her little brother in play, or to look upon the familiar things that she loved so much. Oh, why do we have to give the darling child up?"

" I cannot tell you, May, but just put your trust in God, and all things will work together for good."

" That might be well enough for good people to do, but I am not good enough. It just makes me mad to think Lulu has to be so far from home."

" You are not as bad as you think you are, May. I know you are hot-headed, and very impulsive, but you are no worse than lots of other people. There was the Apostle Paul, a fiery young man going down to Damascus, breathing out threatenings and slaughter against the disciples of God. His heart was hot within him; it burned with rancour and cruelty; his breath was flame. The volcano of his breast heaved and swelled, and poured its streams of fire on every side. When lo ! a light of overwhelming brightness burst upon his astonished vision. Awe-stricken and amazed he fell to the ground. While prostrate in the dust he heard a voice saying unto him, ' Saul, Saul, why persecutest thou me ?' In the midst of his amazement he cried out, ' Who art thou, Lord ?' The answer was, ' I am Jesus whom thou persecutest.' Looking up and beholding the glorious personage, his heart yielded; the adamant broke, and humbled he cried out, ' Lord, what will thou have me to do ?' "

Now the great apostle saw for himself that he was a poor sinner before God. As soon as it was told him what to do he went to work. Now, May, if you only will break that stubborn will of yours, and as Paul of old, cry out, ' Lord, what wilt thou have me to do ? ' then your pathway will be more bright."

" No doubt it would, but for some cause unknown to me, I have no feeling in that direction."

" Strange, strange, indeed, it is May, for one who so needs the blessed Savior's aid to treat the subject so indifferently."

" I know it is, my dear friend. I have sometimes longed for that blessed joy that christians tell of to shine into my poor misunderstanding heart. But in just one moment all is dark. I must be worse than any one else who ever lived, for almost every one, both saint and sinner, seems to grasp the idea of a bright, beautiful world beyond, where we can meet and clasp the hand of those we have loved so well, and dwell in peace and happiness forever. Oh, my heart hopes that it may be so. Have I not ties that bind me to such a hope as this ? But then all with me is dark. Some way, I cannot understand. You may think me jesting, but I am not. Oh ! how sorry I am that this is so."

" Well May, I will not give you up. I know in some way all will be well."

" You may not believe me," said May, " but I am honest. Oh, yes, I love the truth, the blessed truth. My soul fairly thirsts for it."

" Yes, May, I do believe you. One thing I have

always noticed in you is truthfulness. But I am puzzled to know why this should be so."

" My soul," said May, " longs for rest, for peace, and happiness, but I cannot find them. Sometimes there is a wave of pleasantness that sweeps across my troubled mind, and then again all is dark."

" Pray, dear May, pray that God will bring you into the light. The Savior invites, heaven says come, friends beckon you, oh, why do you not see the joyful light ? "

" Forgive me, my dearest friend, but I cannot see the light. Glad indeed would I be if I could tell you that I could. What little I have, all I could do, I would gladly give to have it so. You say to pray, this I have done. I have wrestled like Jacob of old, but unlike him, I did not prevail."

" Well, May, God only knows why this should be so. Yet all his ways are right. Trust him, only trust him. Even if thy soul is overwhelmed with darkness; light will surely dawn."

" My heart goes out for my dear brother's children. I long to fold the little darlings in my arms and shield them from all of earth's care. But here I am as one petrified. What can I do ? No home; not even for myself, and with but little of this earth's means. Oh ! it is hard to be poor. If I had wealth at my command, then I could do something; but here I am. I can suffer, and that is all. When I think of the days that are passed, childhood's happy days, when our family gathered around the fireside and watched with anxious joy to see Lulu take her first steps, I can see the little curly-headed girl with those laughing, sparkling eyes, and then, oh, then, all is blank."

" I, too, May, can remember those little baby eyes of Lulu's which would follow you wherever you moved. Sometimes her little lip would tremble as if her heart was full of fear."

Letters came and went from Lulu to May. Although separated with so many miles between them, yet the love for each other burned in each breast.

May now constantly met with changes as did also Lulu. The change with both from the country's sweet balmy air to the proud ways of city life, wrought changes in both. Lulu's uncle kindly sent her to school, and her aunt spared no pains in trying to educate her in the ways of city life, that she might grow up to be an ornament in the home where she dwelt. But although they were kind, the child constantly sighed for her far away eastern home. Her aunt once said to me, " we loved Lulu, and tried to make things pleasant for her, but all we could do she would not call our house home. I could not blame the child," said her aunt. " I could only compare her feelings to the poor Indian who was taken by the white people, and although they were kind to him, yet his language was:

"Take me back to my home in the far distant west,
To the scenes of my childhood, I love far the best,
Where the tall cedars are, and the bright waters flow,
To the scenes of my childhood, white man let me go."

"Well," said I to her aunt, "I know you were good and kind to Lulu, but the impressions that are made on the mind of a child are as lasting as is our mind. An eminent man once said, 'give me the first eight years of a child's life to make impressions on, and you may have all the rest.' This plainly shows how important are the early teachings of a child."

May God in his infinite mercy protect the child of a vain or indolent parent. I know a son, a bright and noble young man with an intellect unsurpassed by any one whom I ever knew, who was by a proud, vain, and ambitious mother, educated as a violinist, which education was commenced even before the boy was old enough to know good from evil. She loves to see him flattered in the giddy ballroom. She wants him to appear as an accomplished musician, and although to-day he stands as one of the finest violinists in the state, yet it placed him in the way of temptation that he was not able to resist. Now he sees his condition; he, so bright, so noble, so good, and knows full well that he is on the downward road. When he was fully awakened to his condition, he said "oh mother, dear mother, you have made an idol of me. I am going down to ruin. I cannot resist the temptations I am thrown into. You longed to see me accomplished, but I am ruined, I am ruined! Oh, mother, dear mother, pray for me; your boy; your first born." With wringing hands and bleeding heart, and tears that must forever flow, his mother exclaimed: "Oh, my boy, my precious darling boy! I cannot give you up. I have longed to see your name written with those of noble men. My bright, my noble boy! And has it come to this? Oh, yes, I am to blame. Before your little prattling tongue could utter yes, I said it must be so. Oh my boy, my darling, thou art all the world to me."

Now who, I would ask, shall answer for his sin? the boy or the parent? I fear you will have to answer "both."

No wonder dear little Lulu could not forget her childhood's home. Although not as grand as her uncle's fine residence, yet it was where she first beheld the light of day; where she had joined in the merry sports of childhood's happy hours; where she had, together with her little brother. gathered the wild flowers that bloomed near by, Where she had wandered among the tall grasses that grew in the meadow between her father's and grandpa's house. There were many things in the city that she loved, but her childhood home she loved the best. She oft longed for the pure, sweet air, and the fragrant odor of country life, and to play with her brother and little mates.

Her uncle and aunt observed her earnest long-
ing to get back to her home and friends, and as
one year had rolled away, and still she seemed dis-
contented, they thought it best to send her home
again. At first it seemed to dazzel her imagination to think of again seeing her friends once
more.

"Well," said her uncle to his wife, "I think we
had better write to May, and learn what she thinks
about it. You know she is more capable of taking
care of the child than Jane is." And then he
added, "oh dear me! what will ever become of
Jane? She is more of a care than the children
are."

"Yes," said his wife, "May will do all she can
for Lulu. I do wish May was muried, then Lulu
would have a good home."

"Yes, but then her husband might not be willing
to have her," said he.

"Don't fear about that. May would have that
in the bargain."

"Do you wish to return home Lulu and see your
Aunt May and Charlie?"

"Oh, yes, dear uncle and aunt, you have been
very kind to me, but I cannot help it. I long to
go home and see dear Aunt May, mamma, little
brother Charlie and all of the rest. It seems like
a dream, but I hope it may be so. Arrangements
were made and Lulu started at once back home.
Her uncle wrote May to meet her at the train.

May could scarcely wait until the day arrived for Lulu to get home. At last the day came. Ward and May were at the train, but no Lulu came. The next day they again went to the station and still no Lulu came. May now became excited, and with lightning speed she sent a dispatch: "*Lulu is not here. Did she start? If so something must have happened.*" Her uncle received the dispatch, and although much exited, yet dared not reply by telegraph, as he had sent the child, and he knew May would be almost frantic. He said to his wife, "it is very strange, but surely nothing serious has happened or we would have heard of it by this time. Perhaps the train by some carelessness had to lay over one or two days."

One evening shortly after this, as we were sitting around the comfortable fireside at Ward's house, there was a gentle rap at the door. Ward joyfully exclaimed: "Oh! if here is not Lulu." The darling little girl fairly danced into the house, so glad was she to get back home. Charlie and Ward's children clapped their hands and shouted: "Oh, Lulu has got home! Lulu's got home!" All was joy and excitement. May folded the little girl in her arms and pressed her to her heart. We now inquired of the child why she had been so long in coming. She said there had been some mistake in her taking the right train, which caused her to have to lay over two days on her trip home. I could plainly see by May's looks, although greatly pleased at Lulu's return home, that something troubled her very much.

When May and I were alone, I said to her, "you are very glad to see Lulu are you not?"

"Of course I am," said May, but I am very much bothered to know just where she is going to have a home. You know Ward has all the family that he should have."

"Yes, May, that is so. Lulu ought to have a home, where she could be well educated. You know she is a frail child and could not stand many hardships." The thought then came to me, that if May would get married, she could give Lulu a home that would free her from the world's cold frown. So I said, "May, why don't you get married? then you could give Lulu a home."

"La! me! Me get married! Who would I marry?"

"Now May, there is young LaMarr. Why don't you marry him?"

"What are you talking about? He would not have me. He is mad at me," said May.

"No wonder he is mad at you. You act in a way to make him mad at you. Has he not stood by you in the hour of trouble? At the death of your mother, father and brother, also at the parting with little Lulu, who was so ready to sympathize with you as he? And I have always noticed if you wished to go any place he will either take you himself or provide a way for you to go. Is that not so?"

" He has been good," said May, " but then———
" But what ? " said I. He is a good fellow, and
would be good to Lulu. You would be much
happier if you could have Lulu with you. May,
the trouble with you is your hot-headed disposition."

" You are always scolding me about my disposition. I have just the disposition God gave me, (if
there is a God, as you seem to think.")

" Well, May, I only talk to you for your own
good. Would you not like to have a home of your
own, so you could keep Lulu with you ? "

" I would like very much to have Lulu always
with me. She is the precious gem that binds me
to earth."

The next day after Lulu arrived home, Ward
and May took her to see her mother, and as I was
visiting Ward's folks, I thought I would go along.

Her mother seemed somewhat pleased at Lulu's
return, but said, " I have made arrangements with
friends of mine to take Lulu to keep as their own
child. They are coming here to-day to make
arrangements about taking her."

At this a sad look swept over Lulu's face, and
she could hardly speak. In a short time a buggy
drove up and an old gentleman and lady got out.
" Oh ! there they are," said Jane. " Now Lulu you
must act nice, for it will be a good place for you.
I hope you will please them."

When they came into the house, Jane said, " I

am glad you came to-day, as Lulu is here, and can go right home with you." At this tears began to stream from poor little Lulu's eyes. The thought of again being sent from home was more than the poor child could stand.

"How you act!" said her mother. "You ought to be ashamed of yourself. Don't you know it will be better for you to go?"

"I think," said the lady, "this child is rather small. I want a girl that can do my kitchen work, washing, ironing, and the like. I aint one of 'em that believes all a young un is for is to be sent to skool. I larnt to work and that is what I want a young un for."

I now took notice of the old folks. They were very queer looking people. They talked very old-fashioned, and plainly showed that they had never learned to do anything but hard work. No wonder that poor Lulu did not want to go with such looking people.

"Now, Lulu," said her mother, "I want you to go like a lady."

Poor Lulu could not speak. She looked at May through her tears.

"I think," said May, "you ought to be willing for Lulu to make a visit first. You know she has been away from home a long time."

"I think," said her mother, "she had better go."

At this, the gentleman, at whose house we were, spoke up and said: "I think it is a shame to send the child away again so soon without having had time to make a visit."

I was very glad he said this, because he was a gentleman, and felt sorry for Lulu.

" Well," said the old lady, " I do not think the child will suit me anyway. She is too small and looks to me like one of the kind that is more fitted for the pianar than the kitchen."

The old man said to his wife, " I like the looks of the little girl. I would like to have her live with us."

" Oh, yes, I expect you would like to have her sitting around making a lady of herself. But I want you to understand I want a girl for the kitchen."

Lulu's mother seemed very much disappointed. Poor Lulu came and stood near May, as if she was afraid of being taken away again. After they were gone Lulu said, " I am so glad they have gone. I was afraid of them." I did not wonder at her being afraid of them. I noticed a flash of May's dark eyes as she pressed Lulu near her heart, and I said to myself, May has some idea in her head. I afterwards found out that idea.

We cut our visit rather short. I said, " is Jane not a queer mother to be so anxious to send her child away again so soon? I have always looked upon a mother's love as the purest type of love, but I am learning that this is a strange world, or at least that there are strange people in it. Poor little Lulu seemed glad to get away. The child fairly clung to May as if she was afraid some unseen hand would snatch her from her friends. I felt sorry for the poor little girl for just then I could see no prospect for a good home for her. After we had returned to Ward's, we all discussed the question of a home for the child. After we had retired to bed May held Lulu in her arms while hot tears streamed down her cheeks. " Lulu now is nearer and dearer to me then ever before," said May, " since her own mother seems to care nothing for the dear, precious child."

Chapter XVI.

The next time I met May she handed me a paper, which upon reading I discovered to be a marriage certificate.

"Why May, you surprise me! So you married at last. Oh, I am so glad! Now you can give Lulu a home."

"Yes," said May, "I think Lulu and I have been without a home long enough."

Just then a friend of mine came up and began to talk with me, so May left us and passed up the street.

"I am perfectly surprised," said I, "did you know that May was married?"

"Yes," said my friend, "I just heard of it. I have always said that May would marry young La Marr."

"I have laughed considerably at them," said I, "they are both so queer. Half of the time they would not speak to each other, and still in case of trouble La Marr would do anything he possibly could for May. You know May is one of those impulsive girls that must have her own way."

"Yes," said my friend, "I know she is, yet May has a good heart, after all."

"I always thought," said I, "that May enjoyed

11

La Marr's foreign accent, and liked his quick and active way. You know, I suppose, that he is of French descent, did you not?"

"I think I did know of it," said my friend.

The next day after they were married La Marr took May to his home. He had not wealth, yet he had a comfortable home. One thing I will say for May was, she did look well to the ways of her household. The love of long ago now filled her heart. May and her husband gladly welcomed Lulu to their home. The little girl who had not known the comfort of having a home with those she loved most, now felt perfectly free to act and do as she wished. Sad indeed it is to feel the loneliness of having no true home. This is bad in middle life but much worse in childhood. Lulu played and romped with those she loved, and made warm friends with kitties, pigs, chickens, and everything that roamed about the place.

With May and her husband, as with Mildred and her husband in J. G. Holland's "Mistress for the Manse," there was a difference. A difference that no doubt they both felt as long as life lasted. But nevertheless, their home to me was one of the loveliest homes I ever knew. At my first opportunity I called and found them very comfortably situated. The house was one of those old-fashioned one story frame houses, painted red on the outside, trimmed in white. The inside was painted blue. It was one of those dear old houses, substantially

built, and rather fine for its day, that will live in
my memory after they have all crumbled into decay. I learned from some of the old settlers that
the house had been built over forty years, yet it
still retained quite a respectable appearance. I
found May busy at work and little Lulu at play. I
read in May's dark eyes the happiness that filled
her breast. The house was neat and tidy, everything appeared nice. It was the most pleasant
time in May.

"Well May," said I, "it seems good to see you
so pleasantly situated in a house of your own."

"Yes," said May, "I am very happy, because I
now can have Lulu with me. I have longed to
have the little girl, so I could see about her education, and I am very anxious that Lulu should be
well educated."

"Yes," said I, "and you live near a school house
I notice. You have a very pretty home, it is so
pleasantly situated on such a sightly elevation;
just my ideal of a country home."

"We do not possess wealth," said May, "but
what is better still, we do enjoy health, and now I
can take care of dear little Lulu."

"Is your husband willing to keep Lulu?"

"Oh, yes," said May, "he thinks as much of
Lulu as do I, and he is very kind to us both."

"Let us go out and look around the yard," said I.

As we passed out the door I noticed that it was
only about a hundred or a hundred and fifty rods

to Ward's residence, the home of May's girlhood. Their houses stood facing each other.

" It makes it very nice," said I, "for you and Ward to live so near each other, as you are the only two of your father's family left."

" Yes, indeed it is. I can now run over there as often as I please. It also makes it very nice for Lulu, as she now can see her little brother Charlie as often as she likes."

" Oh, yes," said I, "your brother Ward has Lulu's little brother Charlie. That is rather strange ; just one girl and one boy left in each of your father's and William's families, you have the girl, he the boy."

" Yes," said May, "William gave Ward little Charlie just a short time before he died."

Then we walked up and down in the garden. There were currant bushes, grape vines, fruit trees in bloom, flowers adorned the walks, and sweet odors permeated the air. The melody of the wild songster came floating in silver tones on the perfumed breeze. It seemed a hallowed spot.

" Well May," said I, " how happy you should be for all the blessings God has given you."

" I am happy, indeed, in my new home, for be it ever so humble, there is no place like home."

Turning to Lulu I said, " Well, little girl, I suppose you like to live with your Aunt May ?"

Lulu had been playing and running up and down the walks, her curls thrown back, her cheeks aglow, and those large, expressive eyes, that I fail to describe, sparkling with delight. " Yes, I guess I do," came the answer, "I now am going to live always with Aunt May. She says I can."

" Had you not rather go and live with me ?"

" Oh, I want to live with Aunt May." Then the child went on to tell a lot about her pet dog, her kittie, and a little black-eyed pig, which as she expressed it, was just as fat as it could be. Then nothing would do but I must go with her to see the chickens, which she seemed to think were very fine pets. The horses also were favorites with Lulu, and in fact every animal on the place seemed to know and love the little girl.

" Had you not rather live with your mother ?" said I.

" Oh, poor mamma is so queer, and Aunt May and grandma have always cared for me. Willie was mamma's baby, and I was grandma's, but now I am Aunt May's. Is that wrong ?"

Shortly after May was married she commenced sending Lulu to school. It always did me good to see the little girl on her way to school. She was so earnest, so active, so bent on learning. Sometimes she would stop and watch the little birds flit among the trees and nothing hurt her more than to have the boys injure the little birds. I saw her one day with a poor little wounded bird. She tried to put some water and crumbs into its little mouth, but the little bird was too far gone to either eat or drink. Then with tear-stained cheeks she carefully gave it to a friend that he might cease its pain. Lulu made rapid progress in her studies. Her teachers loved her because she was always obedient. There never was a more cheerful, contented little girl than Lulu. She went to school every day, and May was very careful not to keep her out, for, said she, "it is of no use to keep a child out of school one day and send it the next. I want Lulu to have a good education, and if we do not begin while she is young, there will be no use. I also want her to have a musical education, for I believe she has a fine talent in that direction, and she is a good singer."

" Yes, I know she is. Are you going to teach her to work?"

"Of course I shall, when she is old enough, but Lulu is smart and it will not take her forever to learn to work."

" May, I believe you work too hard."

" Oh, I guess not. I would love to see things glitter."

May, as she ever had been, was still nervous, impatient and active, but she at any time would gladly deny herself for Lulu. Nothing gave her such joy as for Lulu to be successful in her studies. Lulu now had attended school one or two terms since May was married. The little girl began to forget the lonely days that she had spent so far from home and friends. She now looked upon her Aunt May's home as her true home. She now felt free from the chilly thought of ever leaving May.

CHAPTER XVII.

To return to Jane. She remained the same careless person she ever had been. No comfort to herself or to any one else. She was not content to stay with her sister, preferring rather to wander around the country associating with the lower classes of people. At last she became acquainted with and married a low, dissipated man, one who could truly sing, " No foot of land do I possess, I am a wanderer in this wilderness."

"The ways of the froward are an abomination in the sight of the Lord." She again took upon herself the cares and duties of a housekeeper. A position she was very illy prepared to fill, now, as before, possessing no faculty for making her home pleasant. They lived in a little shanty within one or two miles of a town, near one of those low grogeries where the very lowest class of men drink, fight and gamble.

" Well," said Jane to her husband, " I am lonesome here, and I want to go and get my girl to stay with me."

" Have you a girl ? I never knew that before,'' said he.

" Yes, I have a girl, and I am going to have her, too."

" Well, old woman you had better not be too fast. I don't know as I want her here."

" I don't care whether you want her or not, I am going to have her," said Jane, " and if you get drunk it will scare her almost to death, for she never saw any one drunk."

" Oh, so, so! She, I suppose, is a young goddess that I will have to fall down and worship! We will see about that. If I want to drink I shall drink, for all of you or your girl either."

" Well, I am going to get her any way. I might as well have her help as May. May is her aunt. I can't bear her anyway. My folks all stick up for May, but I will show them that I am the girl's mother, and I am going to have her."

" Do as you please, old gal, and I will let you," said he, " I will get old Davidson to take you and go after her." Mr. Davidson was the man Jane's husband was working for.

Now if Jane had used any judgment at all, she would have been glad to have let Lulu stay where she was.

" Well Davidson, I came over to see if you would take the old woman after her girl?"

" Do you mean your wife?" said Mr. Davidson.

" Yes," said he.

" I did not know your wife had a girl," said Mr. Davidson.

" Neither did I until this morning."

"Do you know whether the people who have the child will be willing to give her up?"

"They will have to, my woman says. They are not good to her."

"I am afraid we may have trouble about getting the child, and as you are not situated to care for a child, I think you had better let her be where she is," said Mr. Davidson.

"Oh! if you are not willing to go, I will get some one else."

"I am willing to go," said Mr. Davidson, "but I am afraid it will not be as well for the child. But I will go over and see your wife. I may persuade her to let the child remain where she is until you are better situated to take care of her."

"Oh, you can go over, but it will do no good, for she is going to have her dead or alive, one of the two."

"I guess she is not as ferocious as that, is she?" said Mr. Davidson.

"I came over," said Mr. Davidson, "to see you about your little girl. Your husband says that you have one that you wish to go after. Do you not think the child better off where she is? You are not situated well to have her here."

"I am going to have her, any way. She lives with her aunt, who is not good to the child. She knocks and kicks her around," said Jane.

"Is her aunt your sister?"

" No, she is William's sister, he was my first husband."

" Well, I suppose I will have to go, but I really dread it," said Mr. Davidson. " How far is it to where the child lives ?"

" It is near T———."

" It will be a long drive, for that is over twenty miles from here. Well, I will go and get ready, and you had better wrap up pretty warm, as it is very cold."

Mr. Davidson came directly with his horses and sleigh, and they were soon on their way. " I am very much afraid you are doing a bad thing for your child," said Mr. Davidson. " You know your husband drinks."

The sleighing was fine although it was very cold. Mr. Davidson did not enjoy the trip, as he was so afraid that it was not best for the child for he well knew that Jane was not well situated to take care of her.

" We will soon be there," said Jane, " I am well acquainted with the roads."

" What will you do if her aunt refuses to give the child up ?"

" I am going to have her," said Jane, " at the risk of my life. I did once strike that good-for-nothing May, and came near breaking her arm. She carried black and blue marks for weeks and weeks."

" Oh," said Mr. Davidson, " I hope you will have

no trouble to-day. Of course I know nothing of either the child or her aunt."

" Well, I know both of them," said Jane, "and I expect to have trouble, but I don't care if I do. If I strike her this time I hope I can break her arm, or head, one of the two."

" You had better be careful or you might get yourself into trouble."

" I am not afraid of trouble," said Jane, " I would like to kill her. Lulu is my child, I am her mother and I am going to have her to-day."

" Well, here we are," said Jane.

" Is this the place ?" said Mr. Davidson.

" Yes, this is where May lives."

" A pretty place," said Mr. Davidson. "You go in ; I had rather not go."

" Oh, I guess you are afraid to go," said Jane, " but I am not one of the afraid kind."

Jane tore into the house like an infuriated tigress.

" I came," said she, " after Lulu."

It happened to be Lulu's birth-day, and May had just made her a present of a gold locket and several other little things. Lulu was that day expecting to have a nice time.

" Oh, I do not want to go! I do not want to go!" cried Lulu. " Why did you come ? Oh ! ma, let me stay with Aunt May."

" No, I want you to go. You are my child, and

I might as well have your work as for May to have it."

" Oh ! Aunt May, let me stay with you. I cannot go ! I cannot go !"

" Dear, darling Lulu, she is your mother. I cannot keep you if she wants you to go."

" Who is the gentleman in the sleigh ? Is that your husband ?" said May.

" No," said Jane, " that is old Davidson. He is the man my husband works for."

" Well," said May, " I will go and have him put up his horses and have some dinner. It is very cold to-day." She then stepped to the door and addressed Mr. Davidson : " Come in and get warm and have some dinner."

" Oh, I guess we will not stop long," said he.

" Come in and get warm ; you must be very cold," again said May.

Mr. Davidson hitched his team, and came into the house. Being an intelligent man, he saw at once that the child was very much better off with her aunt. Things were neat and tidy, and a home-like appearance seemed to prevail. Lulu did and said everything she could to have her mother let her stay, but nothing would do but the child must go. May packed dear Lulu's trunk, putting in the little dresses and clothes she had so carefully made, while tears dropped upon them almost like rain.

At last things were ready. May went with

them to the sleigh. Poor little Lulu cried and begged to stay, but nothing would do but she must go. The child had known so little about her mother for so long she was almost afraid of her. As she had become very queer looking, and as she lacked every quality that goes to make a noble mother, I was not surprised at the poor little child.

Said May to Mr. Davidson, "If the child gets too homesick, I hope you will see that she can get back home."

" I will do all I can for the child," said he.

As the sleigh drove away poor little Lulu said, " Oh, why did you come after me ? I do not want to go. I want to stay with Aunt May. I want to go to school. Oh, dear, dear, what shall I do? Take me back, please do!" Appealing through her tears to Mr. Davidson.

" Poor little girl, do not cry," said Mr. Davidson, " I will do all I can for you."

" Oh dear, dear, I do not want to go. I cannot go !"

May watched the sleigh as they drove away, and then returned to the house feeling, as Coleridge expresses it :

> "Like one that on a lonesome road
> Doth walk in fear and dread."

She could but feel that the change was one that would involve the poor child in sorrow, misery, and disgrace. The house seemed lonely indeed with-

out Lulu. There are times in life that we are surrounded by sorrows that are worse than death.
When we lay our friends in the grave, especially
in childhood, we know it is the end of their suffering. Not so when we see a frail, helpless child
placed in a position that we know can but result
in suffering and sorrow.

" Where is Lulu ?" said May's husband when he
returned home.

" Oh, Jane came to day and took her away."

" For mercy sake ! And you let her go ?" said
he.

" Well, what could I do ? You know she is her
mother," said May.

"Ah ! there is the trouble. But what has she
ever done for the child ? Did Lulu want to go ?"

" No, the child cried and begged to stay, but
Jane insisted that she was her mother, and that
she must go."

" If Lulu stays there long she will go just as
little Willie went. She was his mother, also," said
May's husband.

" Well," said May, while tears streamed from
her eyes, " I am afraid if poor, darling Lulu stays
there long we will never see her again. She will
be exposed to all kind of bad influences. Jane
had as lieve send her to that low grog shop, and
no doubt she will be sent there after beer for her
dissipated husband."

"I would not have let the little girl go. It is a

shame that such a nice child as Lulu should be in such company, mother or no mother. Jane has always been a disgrace to every one who ever had anything to do with her."

"Yes," said May, "her own dear brother, good and noble man that he is, could never do anything with her."

"No, indeed," said LaMarr, becoming somewhat excited, "nor an angel from heaven could do no more with that woman than with a cannibal. I cannot understand why such a woman was ever created, unless it was to show to the world that not every one who bears the sacred name of mother is entitled to it. Mother! That name to me so dear! Dear to me because the one who bore that name for me would gladly have sacrificed her own life for mine. Poor Lulu little knows the true meaning of that word. This is why the child is so dear to me."

"Poor little girl," said May.

"I never will take another child who has a father or mother living," said LaMarr.

I now saw they were both so excited and disappointed that I thought it time for me to say something, so I remarked to May's husband, "Oh, you could not be so cruel as that could you? If every one would say, and stick to it, that they would not take a child having a living father or mother, what would become of the many thousands of poor little and worse than orphan children like

Lulu ? Lulu would no doubt long ago have been in her grave, if no one but her mother had taken care of her."

" Yes," cried May, "and the poor little child would have been better off than she now will be to be beaten and knocked around by Jane and her drunken husband."

" Well," said I, " it is very bad for Lulu. I cannot imagine what will happen to the child if she remains long with her mother. I very much fear she will go to ruin."

"Oh dear me," said May, " to think of Lulu being raised in ignorance, and having no advantage for school is more than I can stand. Better would it have been for the child never to have been born than to be raised as she now will be."

CHAPTER XVIII,

At the home of Jane there was another scene. A poor, miserable hut, her husband a rough look- ing man, with dishevelled hair, and features that made a person stand aghast, presenting to the eye of a keen observer a person of the lowest and most debased character. Poor little Lulu, half fright- ened to death, feared to enter this dismal place. To look upon such a place and call it home, was more than the poor little child could stand. She clung to Mr. Davidson. "My heart fairly bled," said he to a friend, "for that nice little girl."

"Oh! ma, let me go home with Mr. Davidson I do not want to stay here."

"No, you must stay with me," said her mother.

"Let the child come over to our house as often as she likes," said Mr. Davidson. I think my wife can reconcile the child."

"I will go home with you if you will let me," said Lulu. "Oh, please let me go, I am afraid to stay here. I will work for you."

Mr. Davidson was overcome by the innocent pleading of the poor little child. "If you will not let her go now, you must let her come soon. You should understand that the child is not accustomed to things as they are here. She is homesick, and

12

that is one of the worst kinds of sickness," said Mr. Davidson.

"She is no better to stay here than I am," said Jane.

Mr. Davidson growing indignant replied, " Yes, it is different. You came here because you wanted to, and are satisfied. This poor child you have taken from a good home. I think the cases quite different.

" Well, she is my child, I am her mother, and I am going to have her help me. I might as well have her help as for May to have it."

" Aunt May does not make me work hard," said Lulu.

" You had better shut up," said Jane. " You always stick up for that trifling May. If I had a mother I would treat her as such; children now-a-days have got above their parents. It is a ridiclous shame, is it not?"

" Well," said Mr. Davidson, " there is a great difference between parents. This child, as you say, has not been with you much of the time; you seem like a stranger to her; no wonder the child is afraid."

About this time some of the drunken rioters were coming from the grog shop.

" Well, I must go home," said Mr. Davidson. " Take good care of the little child."

Lulu looked after him with tears streaming down

her pale cheeks. "Oh! ma, I am so lonely here, can I not go to Mr. Davidson's."

" No, you must stay with me."

Jane's husband was a cross, burly man of whom Lulu was afraid, and his companions who frequented the grog shop were of such a character that the child thought that she surely had got among heathens.

" I never felt so sorry in my life for a child as I did for that little girl," said Mr. Davidson to his wife when he got home. " If I had known how the child was situated I would never have gone after her. But Fred's wife (Fred was Jane's husband) said that the people who had her were not good to her, so I thought I would go."

" Oh, that woman is not bright. I thought to myself when you went, if her child had any home at all she was better off than she could possibly be with her," said his wife.

" The child had a good home and her aunt is an intelligent woman who thinks everything of the child. The little girl is one of the nicest little girls I ever saw. The poor little thing begged to stay with her aunt, but nothing would satisfy her mother but to bring her away. The poor child cried almost all the way here. When we got to their shanty, Fred came out. The child, half frightened, clung to me, and no wonder, for Fred always looks frightful enough to scare a man to

death, let alone a child. The child is a pretty, re-
fined looking little girl."

"Poor little thing," replied Mrs. Davidson, " we
must see about her. She may get sick."

Poor, silly Jane had fallen so low that she also
began drinking almost as bad as her dissipated
husband. She found great pleasure in hanging
about the saloon joking with the half intoxicated
men, who were of the most debased character.
Shortly after Lulu's arrival her mother said, "come
Lulu, we will go over to Mr. Kruger's. This was
the man to whom the saloon belonged. Lulu, glad
to get away from the dismal place, readily went
with her mother. But as soon as they arrived at
the place the child saw something was wrong·
The red, bloated faces of the low fellows, their
rough, vile talk, and the sight of seeing her mother
also indulging in the low conversation and drinking the poisonous stuff, half frightened the child to
death.

" Well," said one of the drunken men, " quite a
pretty little miss. Won't you give me a kiss, little
girl?"

Lulu turned pale and began to cry. At this the
low fellow caught the child in his arms and said, ·
" I will soon make you feel better; you must have
some wine." He took a small glass, filled it half
full of wine and tried to pour it down Lulu's
mouth. ˉ The poor little girl fought and screamed,
and giving the fellow a scratch in the face, she

grabbed his hand and bit it so he let her fall on the floor. Poor little Lulu lay unconscious at his feet. At this her mother rushed up and said, " you have killed my child."

Water was poured all over the child which soon revived her. Jane now took the child home, still almost unconscious.

The next morning Mr. Davidson's wife said to her husband, "you must go over and see how that little girl is getting along. I could hardly sleep last night thinking about the poor little child."

" Neither could I, and I am going over and see that woman. I am going to have that child sent back if I have to employ an officer to take her. I feel like one condemned for bringing the child from a good home. She is a sweet little girl and when the poor little thing begged so to stay with me, it touched my heart," said Mr. Davidson, wiping away a tear.

" I don't blame you," said his wife. " Bring the child over here if you can, but I expect you will have trouble with her mother."

" I don't care if I do. She is not capable of taking care of the child, if she is it's mother, and I am going to have something done. I am now thoroughly aroused. There is a law to protect helpless little children and this one needs protection if ever a child did."

" Good morning," said Mr. Davidson, as he entered the dismal abode. Poor Lulu seemed very much pleased to see him. The child looked a shade paler than when he first saw her at her aunt's. "How did the little girl get along during the night?"

"Oh," said her mother, "she cried a good deal. She was so afraid of the men over at the saloon. There was a fight and some of the drunken men made so much noise that it nearly scared her to death."

"Did Fred get drunk?" said Mr. Davidson.

"Oh, he got a little boosey, but you know I am not afraid of him."

"No doubt you are not," said Mr. Davidson, "but this little girl is. She has not been accustomed to such scenes and it is not best for a child to live in continual fear. I think after the child has made you a good visit you had better let her go back to her aunt's, so she can be sent to school. I think it will be better for her, as her aunt thinks so much of her, she will be good to her."

"I don't care if she does go," said Jane. "She has acted so since she has been here that I will be glad when she is gone."

"Let her go over to our house. My wife would like to see the child," said Mr. Davidson.

Lulu was overjoyed to get away from such a dismal house.

"Well," little girl, I am glad to see you," said Mrs. Davidson, "would you like to come and live with me?"

"I would like to go back and live with Aunt May. I was grandma's girl as long as she lived, and now I am Aunt May's."

"Well, little girl, if you want to go back to live with your aunt, I am going to see that you go. I will give you money to go back on the cars. You can make your mother a good visit, then you can go back."

"Oh," said Lulu, "I am so glad! I am so glad! Now I can see Aunt May, and always live with her. Aunt May wants to send me to school all of the time. I wish I could go to-day."

"No, you make your mother a visit, then you can go."

"Oh! you are so good," said Lulu, "clapping her hands, "I now can go home. I am so afraid to stay over where ma stays. I am afraid of that man, and those men that are drinking. I never before saw such work."

Mr. and Mrs. Davidson were very kind to the little girl. They knew she could not stand it long at such a place.

"I was bound to have that child sent back to her aunts," said Mr. Davidson to me a few months afterward, as I happened to meet him. "I felt so sorry when I saw what a good home the poor child had. Of course she could never have been raised any way with her mother."

"Well," said Jane to her husband, after Lulu went over to Mr. Davidson's, "I will be glad to have Lulu go back and live with May. Lulu has always been a headstrong thing. I felt like giving her a good whipping last night. The good-for-nothing thing cried so I could hardly sleep, afraid of those men at the saloon. Who ever heard of such a thing? She just needed a good thrashing, and she will get it, too, if she don't behave."

"I really don't know what you wanted to bring her here for," said her husband. "I thought when I saw you comin' you had brought trouble. She look'd scar't to death, and when she was beginnin' to cry I felt like givin' her a good dab in the mouth."

"My folks, as well as William's have always made a fool of Lulu. They seem to think her a little angel. They have always tried to nose me around, but I guess they have found out that I will do as I please."

"Angel!" said he, "hern is more the nature of an imp. I was just beginin' to make up my mind to give her a good whippin'."

"Oh, you old fool, if you had touched her I would have knocked your head off of your shoulders."

"Well you jist better try that. I ken whip such a thing as you in a jiffy. I don't want your youngun comin' here agin," said he, kicking over a chair as he left.

About one week after Lulu went away, May was out in her door yard. "Why," said she, looking up the road, "if there doesn't come a little girl who looks just like Lulu." Then she put her hand above her eyes as if to take a better view. "Yes," said she, "that is Lulu," and then she rushed to the gate to meet the child.

"Why, my darling Lulu, how did you get back?"

"Oh, that kind gentleman who came with mamma gave me money to come back on the cars. I could not stay there, I was so afraid. Those men over at the saloon drank and made so much noise that I was half frightened to death, I could not help crying so much of the time that ma said she would be glad when I was gone. Oh, dear, how glad I am to get home again. Mamma is never going to take me away again, because I cried so much she got tired of me."

"I am very glad you have returned home, Lulu. School will commence next Monday and now you can go again. I was so afraid that you would have no advantage for school there.·

"There was no school house there, nothing but that saloon, and those wicked men. Oh, Aunt May, that was an awful place. It haunts me yet."

"Why did you not stay at the depot and send for us to meet you, Lulu? You must be very tired for you have walked over three miles."

"I was so glad when I got to town I could not wait, and I knew the road home so well, too. I am not tired one bit. I ran almost all the way.

Everything seemed so nice. Oh, I am so glad I am home again."

"Take off your things, Lulu, and sit down. You now are too excited to feel how tired you are. Where is your trunk Lulu ?"

"It is at the depot. Here is the check, Aunt May. Mr. Davidson said I must take good care of it, for if I lost it I could not get my trunk."

It was hard for Lulu to sit still long. She had to have a romp with her pet kitten and Fido. Said she to them, "I guess you are glad I have got home. It seems like a month since I saw you, you dear, old, fat puffy," said she to her kitty.

When May's husband came back she said to him, " we have a little stranger here."

"Who is it ?" said he. At this Lulu came running out.

"Well, well, if Lulu isn't at home. You little elf. I guess you are glad to get home."

"I guess I am glad. I am always going to stay now. I did not like to stay down there one bit."

"Is it not strange," said May, "that Lulu likes to stay with us so much ?"

"I do not think it is," said I. "Children are like plants. Now you know there are plants to which poor soil or rich soil seems to make no difference. Mullen or burdock do admirably, either on gravelly hillsides or in rich garden soil, but take a rose or a hyacinth and turn it out to shift for itself by the roadside, and it soon dwindles and dies.

Just so it is with children. Some can stand any treatment, while others dwindle and die unless treated kindly. I can plainly see Lulu cannot stand hard treatment. She is like the hyacinth and would soon sicken and die in an uncongenial home."

That evening after the work was all done we gathered around the comfortable fire. I could see that May and her husband were well pleased to have the little girl back. Not so much for their own benefit, because it is no small job to take a child, send her to school and care for, but because they knew it would have been a thing utterly impossible for her to have been well taken care of by her mother. May took the little girl on her lap. The poor child, over weary with her long walk, and the anxiety she had passed through while at her mother's, at once fell asleep in her aunt's arms. Oh, how May nestled the little girl to her breast and looked into the beautiful face of the sleeping child. Her head was a wilderness of curls of a golden auburn, which with the well defined penciling of the eyebrows, the delicate polished skin, and the long silken veil of the lashes that fell over the sleeping eyes made her look like a jewel indeed, too pure for earth. As I watched May's tender, motherly care, and saw the beam of love that sparkled in her eye, I said, " Oh, love is heaven, and heaven is love." "May," said I, " I never saw such love as you have for Lulu."

"Well," replied May, while tears streamed down her cheeks, "the poor child has no one else to love her but me."

"That is so, May. I do not know what would become of the dear little girl if it were not for you. Just think," said I, "of the poor little thing being so unhappy with her mother. But it is not to be wondered at in this case, because her mother neither possesses the love nor the ability to take care of her. Jane is an exception, different from any woman I ever before knew, but I suppose there are others just as trifling as she is."

May then undressed the little girl and tenderly laid her in her bed. The child was so tired and weary that she slept far into the next day before she awoke. She seemed so refreshed and happy at finding herself at home that she fairly danced for joy.

After dinner May said to me, "I do wish I could make Lulu some more school dresses. I do not feel able to buy new ones, as my husband has not the means just now. Don't you believe I could make her some quite respectable ones out of some of my old dresses? She is so small that I believe that I could take the best out of them and make it over for her."

"I think you could," said I.

"Well, I am going to try at least," said May.

I could not help watching her as she went about the task, not altogether an easy one. She cut and planned the very best she could to get out the dresses. She never once seemed to think of herself. She only seemed to think how she might be able to make Lulu comfortable. Out of some old dresses of hers, no longer fit for use, she made Lulu some nice, neat school dresses. Everything May did for Lulu seemed to please the little girl very much. "Oh, aren't those dresses nice, that Aunt May made me? They are just as nice as new," said Lulu when they were done.

CHAPTER XIX.

As May was very fond of those older than herself, she spent many happy hours at her home
with an old christian lady, who seemed to take
much pains to be with her a great deal of the time,
and to talk much on the subject of religion. As
she had great confidence in this lady, it made an
impression on her mind. She began to think,
" can I be mistaken? Is it possible I am all in the
dark? Is there a glorious world beyond?" Oh,
how she longed for it to be so. Her heart and
soul sighed for something better than the cares
and sorrows of this world. The glorious light of
the gospel had begun to dawn in her heart. But
she being desirous of the vain things of life was
all wrapped up in the idea of securing wealth and
making a beautiful home. But the old lady would
not give her up. As a true christian she talked
with her, and wrestled in earnest prayer that God
in his mercy would cause the light to dawn in her
mind, and that she might care less for the vain
things of the world, and more for heaven and
heavenly things. Still May did not yield, her heart
was so hard. She would say, " I have no faith."
Then the lady would tell her that if she would only

believe she would receive faith. But she thought she could not believe.

"My dear friend," said the lady, "there have been others who were just as much in the dark as you are, yet the love of Jesus has dawned into their hearts, and overwhelmed them with glory and brightness."

"Yes," said May, "but it does seem to me that I have done everything in my power, and yet I do not feel the joy that christians tell of. No doubt I have sinned away the day of grace. My disposition is so fiery that it is almost beyond my power to govern."

"Well," said the dear, good lady, "what happens to desolate souls, who thus forsaken cry out to God, is a mystery which you can never fathom until you have been exactly where they are. 'In a little wrath I hid my face from thee for a moment, but with everlasting kindness will I have mercy .on thee, saith the Lord thy Redeemer., 'O thou tossed with tempest, and not comforted, behold, I will lay thy stones with fair colors, and thy foundations with saphire.' You so long for the fine, and vain things of this life, but are they to be compared with these glorious promises?"

"No," said May, "they are not, yet it is hard for me to understand."

"It is a most remarkable property of this old Hebrew literature that it seems to be enchanted with a divine and living power, which strikes the

nerve of individual consciousness, in every desolate and suffering soul. It has raised the burden
from thousands of crushed spirits. It has been as
the day spring to thousands of perplexed wander-
ers. Ah! let us treasure these old words, for as of
old, Jehovah chose to dwell in a tabernacle in the
wilderness, and between the cherubim in the
temple, so now he dwells, and to the simple soul
that seek for him here, he will look forth as of old
from the pillar of cloud and of fire."

" Well, I will try and give this subject much
thought."

But after the dear old lady went home, May's
mind was soon consumed with the care of her
household. She hurried from one thing to another;
she rubbed, and scrubbed, and dusted, in order, as
she expressed it, to have things glitter. She
fretted and worried because things were not just
as she would have them. That night she went to
bed all tired out with the care and anxiety of her
work. She was very nervous, and very ambitious
to make her home beautiful and attractive to those
whom she loved. She was as was Martha of old,
" compassed about with much serving." She had
not, like Mary, chosen that good part that should
never be taken away." She was restless and dis-
turbed in her dreams, and about the dawn of day
as she lay about half awake, she heard as audible
as one could speak, " 'Therefore I say unto you,
take no thought for your life, what ye shall eat, or

what ye shall drink; nor yet for your body, what ye shall put on. Is not the life more than meat, and the body than raiment?" " Behold the fowls of the air; they sow not, neither do they reap, nor gather into barns; yet your heavenly Father feedeth them. Are ye not much better than they? And why take ye thought for raiment? Consider the lillies of the field how they grow; they toil not, neither do they spin, and yet I say unto you that even Solomon, in all his glory, was not arrayed like one of these." She sprang up, "who was that speaking to me?" She now seemed to catch the idea. It was the one " that spake as never man spake." There seemed to come to her mind a peaceful sensation, and she fell to rest in another body than she had retired to bed in.

All through the forenoon she seemed to be in a very thoughtful mood. In the afternoon her dear old lady friend called again to see her. This dear christian lady felt a great interest in May's spiritual welfare.

" Well," said she smilingly, for she well knew that May did not like to have very much said to her on the subject of religion, as she was very irritable at times, "you promised me that you would give the subject of religion much thought yesterday as I was taking my departure."

" Well," said May, " I did. But after you went away I had so much work to do that I did not get time to think much about it."

13

The poor old lady's looks showed that she was disappointed.

"But," said May, "there is one question I want to ask you. This morning, just a little before day-light, were you praying for me?"

"Oh May," said the dear old lady, "I could not give you up. Yes, this morning, long before the break of day, I wrestled with God in pray for you. Oh, May," said she, while tears trickled down her furrowed cheeks, "I can not let your precious soul be lost."

"Well," said May, "I thought you were, because this morning as I lay half asleep I heard audibly, is if some one was speaking to me, the words recorded in Matt., 6 Chap.; 25, 26, 28 verses."

"Oh! that is He! that is He!" said the dear old lady. Oh, now May, you will believe! you will believe! you can't help but believe now. 'The fear of the Lord is the beginning of Wisdom.'"

"Oh!" said May, "is that so? Wisdom? wisdom! Oh! my soul longs for wisdom. I have wrestled in my thoughts for wisdom and knowledge so that I might be able to raise my dear little niece Lulu in the right way. I have ever felt that I was not fit in my own strength to perform such a sacred obligation, but I could not understand how to gain this wisdom. Will you pray for me, that I may be a better, a purer woman, that I may gain this wisdom that my soul so longs for?"

"Yes, I will pray for you; I have prayed for

you for weeks and weeks ; But May this is not all. If you would receive this wisdom you must pray for yourself."

"But," said May, "I am such a great sinner. God does not answer my prayers."

"Then," said the lady, " Fear thou not, for I am with thee; be thou not dismayed, for I am thy God. When thou passeth through the waters I will be with thee, and through the rivers, they shall not overflow thee. When thou walkest through the fire, thou shalt not be burned, neither shall the flame kindle upon thee; for I am the Lord thy God, the Holy one of Israel, thy Savior.' Do you not believe this?"

"It is difficult for me to answer that question. I think that the differences among human beings in the natural power of faith are as great as any other constitutional diversity, and that they begin in childhood. Some are born believers, and some are born skeptics. I was one of the latter. There has ever been an eternal query,—an habitual interrogation-point—to almost every proposition in my mind, even from childhood ; a habit of looking at everything from so many sides, that it was difficult to get a settled assent to anything."

"Well," said the dear old lady, "no doubt the checkered scenes of life that you have had to pass through have confirmed this skeptical tendency."

"I think they have," said May, "but now I am willing to do all in my power to become better and more able to well perform the duties which are mine to perform."

" Well May, you have become very dear to me, your warm impulsive nature, your fiery disposition, has awakened in me a sense of fear for you. The time has now come, I do believe, in your life, when you must give your heart to God or be eternally lost. It is not long after a person wholly gives himself up to God, and humbly cries out ' save, Lord, or I perish,' ' here, Lord, I give myself to thee, it is all that I can do,' and prays to God for strength and wisdom to direct, before the Comforter comes with healing in its wings."

" Well," said May to the dear old lady not long after this conversation, " I now can truly say that light has dawned into my heart. I now would not exchange the joy I feel for all of the vain things of this sinful world. Every morning as I awake, my mind is filled with peace and joy; it is a foretaste of heaven."

" Thanks be to the Great God," said the dear experienced christian lady. " But, May, you must not feel discouraged if you do not always feel this great joy, because there will sometimes dark seasons arise. You know there is no night without a day. Trust God, that is all."

CHAPTER XX.

" Well, May," said LaMarr, one day, "I have
been thinking some of building a new house. I
think we have lived in this old one long enough.
It is the oldest house in the whole country."

"Oh!" said Lulu, " Will not that be nice?"

" We do need a better house," said May, " Yet
we must not be as one of old."

"Ah!" said LaMarr, "I suppose you mean he
who said, 'This will I do, I will pull down my
barns and build greater; and there will I bestow
all my fruits and goods.' "

" You know how it was with him, do you not?"

"Yes, but he had become vain, and made a
boast, and said : 'Saul, thou hast much goods laid
up for many years, take thine ease, eat, drink and
be merry.' "

" But you know God said unto him, 'Thou fool,
this night shall thy soul be required of thee.' "

" But," said I, to May, " It also said, 'So is he
that layeth up treasures for himself, and is not
rich toward god.' It is all right to try and make
ourselves comfortable if possible."

" Well, to-morrow I will engage the masons to
lay the foundation, so that by the middle of
autumn the house can be finished."

It was a fine, warm summer day, the 14th of August, that the masons began laying the stone foundation. That day at the dinner table one of the men said, "Lulu, have you heard that your mother has left her husband?"

"Why! no! When did she do that? I do not blame her," said the child, "for he was the most frightful looking person I ever saw."

"Yes, but," said the man, "why did she marry such a person?" And hastily added, "I suppose Jane has very many queer ideas."

"I wonder what will become of her now," said May.

"Oh!" said the man, "she will soon run across someone else to marry her."

"Well," said LaMarr, "I engaged the carpenters this forenoon to build the house. They will be here as soon as the foundation is done."

"It will seem nice to have a good new house to live in," said Lulu. "This has been a dear old house, but as other people have new houses it will be nice for us also, will it not, Aunt May?"

"It will be very nice," was the reply, "but we must try and appreciate it as we should."

After dinner the men resumed their work. May was busy with her duties, as there was much to do in order to keep things baked up.

"Why was it Aunt May, that I never had a mother like any one else?" remarked Lulu. "I have only known sorrow from my mother."

" I cannot tell you my child,

> ' But a soul untouched by sorrow,
> Aims not at a higher state ;
> Joy seeks no brighter morrow,
> Only sad hearts learn to wait.'

Lulu, although you are deprived of a mother's love and tender care, I will try and do as well for you as I can."

" Oh ! yes, you have always done all you could for me," said Lulu.

As the days had rolled into weeks since LaMarr had been building his house, the time had now come when they were to move into it. One evening after Lulu had come home from school, May said, " Well Lulu, we are moving into the new house."

" Oh dear, how glad I am," said Lulu, as she rushed around helping take things to the new house.

" Well," said May, " I feel as Will Carlton expresses it :

Here the old house will stand, but not as it stood before,
Winds will whistle through it, and rain will flood the floor,
And over the hearth, once blazing, the snow-drifts oft will
　　pile,
And the old thing will seem to be a mournin' all the while.
Fare you well, old house, you're naught that can feel or
　　see,
But you seem like a human being—a dear old friend to me,
And we never will have a better home, if my opinion
　　stands,
Until we commence a-keeping house in the house not made
　　with hands."

CHAPTER XXI.

After wandering around the country for some time there seemed to dawn upon Jane a streak of good luck. A bachelor uncle, just before he died willed her and her brother a large sum of money. Her brother being many hundred miles away from her and feeling very anxious for her welfare, as soon as he learned of the will, sat down and wrote a letter to his sister. "My dear sister," wrote he, "Uncle has been kind enough to will you and I a large sum of money, do now, for mercy sake, try and take good care of yours. You know money is hard to get. Lets now see if we cannot make good use of it. I do hope you will stay single. Please do not think of such a thing as marrying again. You know there are low fellows who would marry you just for your money, and then no doubt leave you as soon as your money is gone. Dear sister, there is your dear little daughter, Lulu. I do wish you would spend part of your money on her. You know she is a very loveable girl. Why not buy her an organ or a piano? You know she has a fine talent for music, and her Aunt May is doing all she can for her. Just now she is not able to buy a musical instrument. No doubt Lulu would make a fine music teacher if she had the chance. You might also help to educate your little son Charley. You will have enough money, which if taken good care of, will be plenty for your own use, and also some to help your children with."

"Well," said Jane as she slammed the letter down, "I suppose brother thinks I have not enough sense to take care of my money. I shall do just as I please with it. It is strange what fools my folks and William's also make of themselves about Lulu. They seem to think her a perfect little angel, while she is nothing but a common child."

"Well," said the lady to whom she was talking, "You know your folks are interested in your children's welfare."

"Yes," said Jane, "they are more interested in their welfare than they are in mine."

"Oh, well," said the lady, "you know the children are young yet."

"I don't care if they are," said Jane. "I shall do just as I like."

And sure enough she did. Just as soon as she came into possession of the money she married a very dissipated fellow, whom she met at a friend's house, and who was almost an entire stranger to her. All of her friends were very much mortified at the way she did. Another thing she did which made it very bad for May and Lulu. She bought a small place about one mile from their home, where they had to constantly come in contact with her dissipated husband. The first time I met Jane with her new found treasure was one time when I was going to a friend's house. I saw her coming, her red ribbons fluttering on the breeze, with portmonie swinging in her hand, and very triumphant indeed, did she seem.

"Well," said I, "this, I suppose, is your new husband, Jane, is it not?" I saw she did not intend to introduce him to me, so I thought I would make myself acquainted.

"Yes," said Jane.

As soon as he learned who I was he tauntingly remarked, "Will you please tell Jane's folks to send her daughter, whom I believe they call Lulu, up so we can buy her a piano?" As he said this I saw an overbearing grin on his face. "I learn they are very anxious," said he, "for Jane to use her money for the good of her children." I at once discovered that he was a very quarrelsome person, I therefore left them and went to my friend's house.

"Well," said my friend, "did you see Jane and her husband?"

"Yes, I saw them," said I. I then told her how tauntingly they had talked about Jane's money.

"Well," said my friend, "Jane might better have spent her money for her poor innocent children than to have spent it on that low dissipated fellow. Dear me, what will ever become of that poor, trifling, silly Jane? Had she used her money as she should, she would have had enough to have helped to educate her children, and plenty to have taken good care of herself. But now it will be squandered. The very day that she married this fellow she bought him a twenty dollar suit of clothes. It is really too bad, now poor little Lulu, and all of Jane's folks must be disgraced by this low drunken fellow."

CHAPTER XXII.

One day, a few months after Jane's marriage,
May saw a man drive up to the gate in an excited
manner, spring from his vehicle, leaving his horse
unhitched, and come reeling towards the house.
May at once recognized the man to be Jane's new
husband.

" Well," said he, " I have run my horse thirty
miles to-day in order to procure a lawyer to have
you and your brother, Ward Montroville, arrested
for cheating my wife's children out of their property."

May being all alone, and knowing the man to be
a very quarrelsome person, and seeing that he was
very much under the influence of liquor, thought
it best to say but little. He, as all drunken men
do, knew that he had very wrongfully cheated his
wife's children by marrying her, and then squan-
dering money which should have been used for
their comfort. He knew that he had done wrong,
and, of course, supposed others to have done the
same.

" I think Lulu is a very lovely girl. I could just
take her in my arms and fold her to my heart,"
said he, " she is so young and pure and sweet.
But then, I suppose it would not look very well

for me so to do, as I am only her mother's husband."

At this remark May felt the blood mount to her face. What, thought she, could I stand it to see my beautiful little niece folded in the arms of such a brutal character as he? No, indeed, she had rather see the pure, innocent girl laid in her grave.

" Well," said the dissipated fellow, " you and your brother had better be careful how you use the children's property, or you will get yourselves into trouble."

Now the property he spoke of was some that had fallen to them from their Grandfather Montroville, and nothing that he or Jane had ever worked to earn. Nevertheless, I suppose, he and she were anxious that in some way they might get hold of it, to squander it also, as they had the other.

After abusing May as much as he was capable of doing, he left.

When he got home Jane said, " Did you get a lawyer?"

" Well," said he, " you just bet I tried."

" What did he say?"

" Oh, the lawyer said I had better mind my own business."

" Business!" said Jane, " well, is it not your business?"

" The lawyer said neither you nor I were capable of taking care of the children, and that we had better let the Montrovilles alone, because the property belonged to them anyway."

"That is just the way everybody makes fools of themselves about those good-for-nothing brats of mine," said Jane.

"Well, old woman, you haint got sense enough to take care of them. Lulu knows more in one minute than you ever knew in your life; besides she is sweet and young and pretty."

"Well," said Jane, "you are just as big a fool as the rest. You are in love with Lulu."

"Well, she is nice, and I love her, too. If you were half as nice I might think a little something of you."

"Yes, that is all you think of me. It was my money you married."

"Yes, it was, and just as soon as it is gone I am going to sea. You know I am an old tar, don't you?"

"Tar or no tar I hope you will get drowned."

"Well," said he, "it ain't the first old fool I married just in order to get a little spending money to buy my rum. You might have known better than to marry a stranger. I think just as the lawyer thought about you. He said an old woman like you ought not to have been so hot to get married, and that the children's father was a nice man, and I believe it, because they are nice children, and one thing sure, I do know, they never took that after you."

"You poor old black fool," if I was a man I would whip you to within an inch of your life."

" You had better bake some more bread," said he, " I tell you, you are a good cook."

" Well, I am as good a cook as you are a farmer."

" See here, old woman, if you expect me to farm you will be mistaken. You know there is a little of your money left, when that is gone I will quit this place to plow the deep blue sea."

" Well," said Jane, " the sooner the better, then I can marry some one else."

" Oh, yes; there is old Cummings, you can marry him, he is running after you every time I'm away from the house."

" Well," said Jane, " it is none of your business who runs after me. He is just as good as you are."

" Well, old woman, it is a great blessing for your daughter that you have not the raising of her."

" I don't care for you nor my daughter either." I intend to have a good time, daughter or no daughter."

" I have been around the world a good deal, and have seen many mothers, but you beat the devil. You care no more for your daughter than you would were she a dog. One thing I do know, if I am an old tar, she is a fine girl."

" You had better stop praising Lulu," said Jane, " I won't stand it. Lulu is no better than I am. May makes a big fool of Lulu, and sends her to school all of the time. She is trying to make a big lady of her, and wants to get her a piano. She had better buy her a washboard and let her play music on that."

" Well, old woman, if she could make as good use of a washboard as you do it would pay. Your washing looks like you had rinsed your clothes in coffee."

" I don't intend to break my back rubbing your clothes," said Jane.

" No, indeed, old woman, I know you don't. You have washed me two shirts in six months."

" Hello? what is that noise I hear?" said a passer-by to a companion. " Oh, it's Jane and her husband fighting. You see he is drunk, and then Jane takes the pains to get up a quarrel with him." " She had better let him alone when he is drunk." " That would not be Jane. You see, she delights to get up a fuss as soon as he comes home, which always ends in a fight.

CHAPTER XXIII.

As I had been called away to spend some time in a different country, I knew but little of the changes of the neighborhood where the Montroville's lived. When I returned I at once went to visit May. Lulu had grown to be a fine girl. In the evening May invited us into the parlor.

"Oh," said I, "did Lulu's mother ever get her a musical instrument as her brother wished her to at the time she fell heir to her money?"

"No, indeed, she did not. But just as soon as I felt able I bought her a piano. You know she has a talent for music, and I believe we should improve the gifts that God has given us."

"Well, Lulu," said I, "can't you play some for me?" She took her seat at the piano, and as her skillful fingers swept the keys of the instrument, playing several pieces of music, she began one of the sainted Longfellow's pieces known as "The Bridge," and as her pure, sweet voice floated through the room, I could not help remarking that it seemed almost impossible that this was the little girl I knew before I went away.

"Lulu has been a very good girl," said her Aunt May. "It has been my greatest desire to try and do right by her."

14

"Well, May, you have had to raise her surrounded by many difficulties."

"Yes, and these have made her still dearer to me. It is ten times as hard to raise a child who has other relatives living."

"Yes, I know it is."

"You know if you do too much for them somebody will find fault. If you do too little, then there will be fault found with you. "But," said May, "I will do as near right as I possibly can. I I am only human, no doubt I shall make many mistakes, but I will trust the Allwise Hand to direct me.

———

One cold stormy evening in the dead of winter, as I happened to be going a short distance to a friend's house, I was somewhat surprised to meet May hurrying along, apparently in great agitation.

"Now where are you going?" said I.

"Have you not heard," said May, "that Jane's husband is very sick and not expected to live?"

"Now, May," said I, "you are not able to go there; you are nearly sick yourself?"

"Oh, I guess I can stand it."

"Well, you may stand it, and you may not. Why did your husband allow you to go?"

"I just heard he was sick. My husband was away, and I knew something must be done for the poor man."

"I think they have abused you enough, and that

you have long ago cleared your skirts of any duty toward them. He is nothing to you."

"He is my dear Lulu's mother's husband."

"Why did you not send Lulu?"

"I could not have done that for anything. You know Lulu takes cold so easily, and her lungs are weak. I never dare to let her expose herself one bit."

"I know she is a frail girl, but May, you are not well."

"Well, or not well," replied May, "I must go."

"If you really must go, I will go with you, as it is getting dark." Therefore we hastened to the dismal abode. As we entered the house the room was dark and dismal. May stepped to the bedside of the poor dying man. He was sitting carelessly propped up in his bed, unable to lie down on account of shortness of breath.

"I just heard," said May, "that you were sick, and have come to see how you are."

"I am glad that you came," said the poor man, extending his poor hand, already turning black from putrification of excessive drink.

"I have brought you some fruits, thinking perhaps you might be able to eat a little," said May.

"I cannot eat now," said the poor fellow.

We at once saw that the poor wretched man's days were nearly numbered. May, after a little hesitation, held up to the dying man the bible; and spoke of the consolation of its doctrine.

"Ah! yes," said the poor man, "my life has been a hard one. I've ploughed the waves of both ocean and sea, and hugged the shore and embarked and prepared for storm. I have seen the whitecaps roll mountains high. I have felt ground swells and got through alright, but one great thing I have neglected. Ah, yes, I have hardly known of such a book all my life, and my associates have been so rough. But once while sick of a fever in a hospital away off the coast of South America, did a noble christian missionary woman give me the blessed bible to read. I there found out it was a good book, yes, the book of books. But you see my early instruction, my wicked associates, my dissipated habits, I could not forget. Oh those missionary women, may God bless their work; they are good and noble women. Before I saw them I had lost confidence in woman kind. You see the women that flocked around the wharfs where we landed were women of the lowest character. But, oh, those good noble women. If I had only heeded their advice. But now it is too late; too late." As the poor man's feeble voice died away, I took notice of the dark and dismal surroundings. There sat Jane, hair uncombed, dress untidy. The house was dirty and very illy kept. It seemed as if demons were in the room.

The next night the poor man died. There seemed to be no other way, but that I should remain alone with Jane on the day the poor man lay a corpse in the house.

" Well," said Jane, " I am glad he is dead. Now perhaps I can have some comfort."

" Why, Jane," said I, " what are you talking about ? "

" Well," said she, " I am talking about just what I mean. I am glad he is dead."

" Well, Jane, will you marry the next man who comes along ? "

" I shall do as I like about that," said Jane.

CHAPTER XXIV,

It had been some fifteen or sixteen years since the school house I have before spoken of was built, and that had ever since been used as a house for the worship of God. Now that the country had become more improved, and things had become more modern, it was thought best to build a church. There were a few faithful christians that had stood together through many dark days of trial and persecution. But nevertheless, they stood heart and hand together, and said we must have a church where we can worship God together, where none can molest or make afraid.

Therefore they appointed a time to meet, and talk the matter over, and appoint trustees. Ward Montroville who was among the leading members of the church, now came forth, as he always did in any good enterprise, and said, " Yes, we must have a church. I will stand an equal amount with any of our brethren." As Ward was the young-, est of the society his remarks pleased the oldest and one of the most wealthy of the members. " I too," said he, " will stand an equal share."

" I will do the same," said another. "And I," said another. At the meeting all of the necessary arrangements were made for building the church.

" Well," said May's husband to her after the meeting, where do you think they want to locate the church ?"

" I suppose they have chosen our place, as it is about the center of the neighborhood, and near the school house."

" Yes," said he, " they would like to build it on the corner east of our house, near the cross roads."

" That would be a very pretty place," said May, " but I very much fear it would make trouble. You know our neighbors who live just across the road, one on one corner and the other on the other corner, do not belong to a church. I very much fear they will object."

" Yes," said LaMarr, " they do. As I was coming home, I met Milton, and never once thought but what he would be glad to have the church there, and I told him about it. I saw he did not like it. He said if we did, he would build a dancing hall on the other corner."

" Just as I expected," said May.

" Well," said I, as I happened to be at May's house, " you have a right to build the church where you like."

" But," said May, " we would not like to cause hard feelings about it. You know, in Job's time, there was a day when the sons of God came to present themselves before the Lord, and Satan came also among them, Job chap. 1 v. 6. I suppose now he has begun his work, you know he always does just as soon as he thinks there is a chance for some good to be accomplished."

And sure enough he went around from heart to heart, and stirred up the people. Some said, that is the right place for the church, others said, " No, we will not have it there." One of the leading members said, " If we cannot locate the church near the corners, where it should be, I shall not give one cent towards it." After Satan had done all in his power to agitate the minds of the people, causing much trouble and dissatisfaction, some-one said, we will appoint a committee to whom we will leave the matter of locating the place for the church, then we must be willing to abide by their decision.

Said one of the leading members of the committee, "I thought I would come early so we could talk over the matter of the location of the church. I am very much in favor of having it near the cross-road, what do you think?" said he, addressing May.

" Well," said she, " I, too, think that a pretty place, but you know it would cause trouble. There is a very pretty and sightly location west of the house, why not have it there?"

" We can never bear the idea," said he, " of having it in any place but the one first spoken of."

" Then," said May, "let us commit it to the Lord. 'Commit thy ways unto the Lord, and He will direct thy path.'"

"I will go up and look at this place you speak of and see about it." In a short time he returned, his face all aglow. Said he, "The moment I stepped on the ground something seemed to impress me that it was the proper place for the church." The committee were not long in deciding the matter, and the church was there located. Nevertheless there were a few persons who had never intended to give one cent, said, "If you had built the church at the corners we would have given you one or two hundred dollars." And yet to-day there stands a beautiful brick church on this sightly location, while the poor man who said he would build the dancing hall sleeps in the silent grave. The Lord's ways are above our ways and his thoughts are above our thoughts.

October has come and among the forests flame out the scarlet branches of the maple, and the beech groves are arrayed in gold, through which the sunlight streams in subdued richness, swathing in purple mists the rainbow brightness of the forests, blending their colors into wondrous harmonies of splendor.

"Well," said one of the trustees, "after so many days of toil and anxiety the church is at last completed. When shall we have it dedicated?"

Ward Montroville replied, "We are having such fine autumn weather, I think the sooner the better."

"Well, then," said he, "we will have it dedicated on next Thursday, if that time suits."

"I think the time very appropriate," said Mr. D——. "We will have to make our arrangements, but I think we can get ready by that time. Brother T—— will preach the dedicatory sermon."

Said another of the trustees, "May the blessing of the Lord still continue with us."

In the morning on the day of the dedication of the beautiful little church, Ward, May, and I went into the edifice for the purpose of making some necessary arrangements for beautifying it with bouquets of flowers. It was one of those lovely days about the middle of autumn, that seems to fill the soul with awe and reverence. Ward had arisen with the morning sun and went forth to meditate. He had labored hard to accomplish the great task of building this house for the worship of God. Many times when discouragements would arise, he felt, like Peter of old, to cry out, "Save, Lord, or we perish," but this morning he came in with his mind softened and glowing. The trance-like calm of earth found a solemn answer within him. His language was, "Bless the Lord, O my soul. O, Lord, my God, thou art very great; thou art clothed with honor and majesty; who coverest thyself with light as with a garment; who layeth the beams of his chambers in the waters; who maketh the clouds his chariots; who walketh upon the wings of the wind. The trees of the Lord are full of sap; the cedars of Lebanon, which he hath planted, where the birds make their nests; as for the stork, the fir trees are her house. O Lord, how manifold are thy works! in wisdom hast thou made them all."

"I have longed to see this day, the day on which we dedicate this house to the Lord."

"Yes," said I, "and now it seems that all things are ready. I am so glad it is such a beautiful day." May was just arranging a bouquet of dahlias, fall roses and some other flowers, when in walked Lulu. Her form seemed slight and frail; her cheeks were tinted with the rose; her appearance one might fancy was like unto a fairy or a sylph. She glided up the aisle and took her seat at the organ and unexpectedly to us her angelic, childlike voice floated through the room. She sang the grand old doxology:

> Praise God from whom all blessings flow,
> Praise him, all creatures here below;
> Praise him above, ye heavenly hosts,
> Praise father, son, and holy ghost.

As the echo of her voice resounded in the room and then died away, my soul caught the fire, a new baptism of love inspired my heart. Ward clasped his hands, and looked away to the fount from which all blessings flow. He fairly shouted glory! The very walls seemed to shout the praises of God. It was a grand, sublime moment. I now look to that morning, although many years have passed since then, as one of the bright spots in my life. The Rev. T——, LL. D., preached from Hebrew 6:5. Subject, "The power of the world to come," and gave a very able address. Lulu Montroville presided at the organ. The singing was subdued and pleasant. The brethren and sisters were very attentive to each other. I felt glad that they were so well situated. I consider their house of worship a perfect little gem of beauty.

> " Together let us sweetly live,
>   Together let us die;
> And each a starry crown receive,
>   And reign above the sky.

CHAPTER XXV.

May and her husband went to a western city to visit LeMarr's folks. They had a delightful time. It was somewhat of a manufacturing town and in it there were large stone quarries. These interested May as she had never before seen any. After spending a number of days taking in many fine sights, viewing the beautiful prairies, they returned to Chicago. Here they visited the exposition, the fair, and many other things of note. While in the city they had their photographs taken. As May's husband was to remain in the city some weeks, they bade each other good-bye, May returning home to see how Lulu and the affairs at home were getting along. Lulu had taken the very best kind of care of things at home, having the house neat and tidy. I thought as May and Lulu were alone I would stay with them a part of the time. One day May said to Lulu, " as to-day is the fair in town, we will go. It may be that our pictures have come. I hope they have, for I want to see if they are good. We will get the horse and buggy and start at once.

As soon as we arrived in town, May said, " come, we will go to the postoffice." We all went in and May received the pictures and a letter from her

husband. We were all delighted with the pictures,
especially Mr. LeMarr's, which was very fine. As
we were passing out of the door, a man stepped
up to May and asked: " Were you not Miss Montroville ?" "That was my maiden name," said
May. She then looked at the man and recognized
William Bryant, the one who had caused her so
much trouble when only a girl of seventeen. She
now looked with disdain upon him. A man who
would forsake the girl he truly loved to marry one
who was wealthy. The love she once bore for him
had now changed into hatred. "I hear you had
the misfortune to lose your wife," said May.
"Yes," said Bryant. " You look to me," said he,
"as you did many years ago."

"Do I ?" said May. "You are so changed I would
not have recognized you if you had not spoken to
me."

"I have met you before," said the man, "but as
you did not know me I did not make myself
known."

"How old you look and how changed you are,"
said May.

"I have had much sorrow. My wife's health
has always been poor, she lingered with consump-
tion for months and months."

"I am sorry to hear that you have had so much
trouble." But I could see by the flash of May's
dark eyes that it was hard to keep her fiery southern disposition down. She could not help looking

with contempt upon a man who had made gold his idol.—James, 5 chap., 3 v.: " Your gold and silver is cankered ; and the rust of them shall be a witness against you, and shall eat your flesh as it were fire."

" I have a pleasant home and a kind husband," said May." Just then May happened to think of her husband's picture that she had just received. " Oh yes!" said she, " here is my husband's picture, you might like to see it."

I saw by the haggard look of the man that he could hardly bear to look at it, as May's husband was a better looking man now than he. I also read in his looks that he saw now his mistake in marrying a woman much older than himself, and a woman he never loved, simply because she had wealth. May had retained her looks, though never very handsome when a girl. If anything she made a better looking woman than a girl. William Bryant presented indeed a sad, pitiful and unhappy appearance, a wreck of humanity. May seemed anxious to leave his presence, we therefore passed down the street leaving him to his own sad reflections.

" Why! Aunt May, how could you treat that poor man so ? I felt sorry for him. I never saw you treat any one so coldly before," said Lulu.

" Never mind, Lulu, perhaps I had a reason for treating him as I did." As soon as I recognized his name the memory of the past came back to me. I well remembered when May was only a young girl and this man had sought and won her heart; and she, little dreaming of the sorrow and pain he would cause her, had placed her entire affections upon him. He had sought her company in halls of mirth and in quiet walks amid shady groves. He had feasted upon her society, keeping her from the company of others who no doubt would have been true to her, and then because she had not wealth, leaving her for another simply because this other one had gold. " You have forgotten all the love you ever had for this man," said I.

" Yes," replied May, " I only feel contempt for him. I do not possess sufficient charity to respect a person of so little principle. I well remember when I took his picture, after I had heard that he had married another, took a last farewell look and cast it into the fire. With it I cast the love I felt for him. I came near also casting my confidence in humanity, and also came near losing my faith in God. Oh! I was so impulsive, I could hardly recover from the shock it gave me. I said to myself I am too noble to keep a married man's picture in my possession, but you remember it nearly took my life." -

" Yes, I do, and when you were showing him your husband's picture I could not help thinking of it, and also I thought that after all, your pathway had been less strewn with thorns than his.

'All things work together for good to them that serve the Lord.'"

"That is so. I have often heard from him but I always heard that he was surrounded by sorrow. His wife's money did not do him much good after all. No wonder he looks so old and haggard. How time passes! It has been seventeen years since I became acquainted with him. I was then just seventeen. I now am thirty-four."

"Now May, don't you see God's plans are true? When you cast his picture into the fire, noble girl that you were, too brave, too noble to keep in your possession the picture of a man you then had no right to idolize, although it nearly took your life, you were then so sad and lonely. But to-day, after the flight of many, many years, you meet him again. You now are happy, while he is sad; you have a pleasant home, surrounded by warm friends, while his home is dismal and lonely. No doubt if you had kept his memory in your heart, and mourned over it, it would not have been as well for you. You did the very best you could to forget the past, although such things are not as easily forgotten as one might think. But it is always best to look on the bright side."

"Well," said May, "I can not complain. I am now very glad that he preferred gold instead of me; have I not a right to be?"

Lulu, after completing the district school, spent some time at one of the leading colleges of the

15

State, and then began teaching school. The first three or four terms of school she taught in her own district where she had been accustomed to go to school. " I think, May, you should be very glad indeed of your success in helping Lulu to get an education."

" Yes, indeed I am. Lulu has improved her time in the best possible way she could."

" I do believe you have done all in your power to help Lulu."

" Well, yes, I have done what I could, but had we been better able to afford it, I might have done more. Sometimes the way seemed very dark, I have so felt my inability to instruct her as I should. You know humanity is weak, no doubt often I have set wrong examples before her, yet it has been my prayer to God that she might be a good and pure woman."

Chapter XXVI.

Lulu did remarkably well as instructor of the young, being only as you might say a scholar herself, teaching the very scholars she had been accustomed to study and play with. Yet her noble and commanding way demanded their respect. They all loved the brave girl. She did so well, and the scholars made such advancement that she soon gained a reputation of being one of the finest instructors in the whole country where she lived. The officers of the village high school, seeing and hearing so much said of her, as one of the best teachers as well as one of the most noble and pure girls in the entire country, engaged her services and placed her as an instructor in the high school as preceptress. In the high school there were fourteen departments. The teacher in one of the departments under her was the daughter of a merchant, the other of a clergyman; both were girls much older than she, who had been raised with a father and mother's tender love. I fairly trembled for Lulu to be placed in such an important position, but the noble girl stepped into the place with the grace of a queen. The first day of the school the officers met, no doubt anxious to see how this young girl would face her situation. They did indeed feel proud, noble men, as they were, to see how well and nobly she performed her task. They looked into her handsome, girlish face and saw within those expressive eyes a gem of earth, pure, and sweet, yet noble and commanding, and as Dickens expresses it: "Her love was the law of the school." She succeeded beyond all expectation, and so gracefully, so bravely did her work that everyone rejoiced. But as the evil one always has to do his work, this was too much for him to stand, so as cunningly as he beguiled Eve in the garden of Eden, he now began his work. Lulu's success aroused the jealousy of the lower classes of the community. There dwelt in the neighborhood a family having two sons. Both of these young men had tried to gain Lulu's affections. This of course she could not allow, as neither were mentally her equal. They then contrived, as they thought, a plan to bring her to ruin and disgrace. They well knew that Lulu's mother was a poor, weak and dissipated, fallen woman. They therefore went to her mother and said: "Why do you not go and show those high toned village people that they are holding a young lady in a position who will see her mother suffer? You apply to the overseer of the poor for help, and show those people what kind of a daughter you have."

Now poor Jane, too ignorant to understand their vile intention, went to the village, became intoxicated, went up and down the streets into dry goods stores, hotels, and other places of business, and proclaimed: "My daughter Lulu, who is teaching in your high school, will not take care of me, and I am suffering." Lulu's mother was a small and very inferior looking person, and with her as with all persons that gradually sink into dissipation, she presented a wild and vacant stare, and was a person who by her looks would at once gain the sympathy of those who did not know her. She also went to the overseer of the poor and said: " I came to see if you will not help me, as I am suffering. My daughter Lulu Montroville is teaching in your high school, but she will not help me." Now the gentleman did not understand the position, and said, " I am astonished. Can this be possible ? Is she such a girl as that, who would let her mother suffer?" and with emphasis, stamping his foot on the floor, "I will see about this; if she is such a young lady as this, I will see about it. You say you are suffering and she will not help you ? "

" No she won't," said her mother. " She dresses and sticks everything on her own back, and that is all she cares for me."

Poor Jane did not understand that she was destroying her own pure girl's name; a girl who was as free from guile as ever a girl was in this world, and one who could no more help being her child than she could have helped being the child born to a king. Nor had Jane in any way been a help to her own sweet girl; only bringing her into this world, and then possessing no faculty to take care of her, but cast her out upon the mercy of a cold and sinful world.

This news swept like wild fire over the town. "Can it be possible our young teacher is letting her mother suffer?" Both the high and the low were astonished. As Lulu would pass up and down the street on her way to her school, and back to her boarding place, she would be pointed out as the girl who was letting her mother suffer. A low fellow, standing with hands in his pockets, pipe in his mouth, and hat on one side of his head, said as Lulu was passing: "There she goes; the gal that is letting her old marm that worked hard to raise her, suffer. She ought to be ashamed of herself. I know she has a purty face, and is plump and well formed, but I never heard of such a disgrace before."

"You!" said a gentleman standing near, "had better be ashamed of yourself for allowing your vile lips to take such a pure girl's name as this young lady's is, upon them. What have you done for your poor mother?"

Lulu had not yet learned what her mother had done, and, as it was the first week of her school. She was very busy in getting it in good running order. A friend of hers, hearing about what her mother had done, thought it best for Lulu to un-

derstand what she had to face. This friend therefore in the best manner she could, took Lulu alone
and said, " Lulu, I have something I want to tell
you. I know it is very hard for you to bear, but
nevertheless, you will have to bear the disgrace."
Then her friend went on and told her what her
mother had done.

" How did she take it?" I asked Lulu's friend.

" Oh! the dear girl's pure, sweet face looked
like the face of an angel, and tears streamed over
her pure blanched cheeks. " What am I to do?"
said she. "Will I have to give up my school?
How can I face my scholars? What will they
think of their teacher to let her mother suffer?
Oh, dear, dear! What will I do? I have tried in
every way to do all possible for my mother.
What a sad thing it is. You know she is not to
blame, poor woman. My uncle, whom I lived with
in the west, said when she was young that she was
one of the brightest little girls he ever knew, but
it is dissipation that has made her so. Oh, dear
me! I have never known a mother's love."

" I know you have not, dear girl, but never
mind, dear Lulu, in the sweet by and by you will
know why you have had to suffer this great affliction. Earth has no sorrow that heaven cannot
heal."

" How, oh, how can I face the world's cold
frown?"

I looked upon the poor girl's frail form, trembling with grief, but could not tell why a girl so young, so pure, so gentle, should have such sorrow. I said to myself, "Thy ways are hard to understand, but Thy paths are peace."

The lower classes seemed to take up the news and hurl it to the breeze, but the better classes, the people of mind and intelligence weighed the matter and found out how the thing stood. Lulu was upheld. The noble christian people would not see a young, frail, and helpless girl crushed by willful slanderers. Hard enough said they it is for this dear girl to bear the sorrow of having such a mother, without having to stand such falsehoods as evil and willful people circulate. " The words of a tale-bearer are as wounds, and they go down into the innermost parts of the body." " He that answereth a matter before he heareth it, it is folly and shame unto him." " Death and life are in the power of the tongue, and they that love it shall eat the fruit thereof." Although some seemed to love to dwell upon the strain, " our young teacher is letting her mother suffer," but the same as ever, " resist the devil and he will flee from you."

Lulu, brave and noble girl, met the trials thrown around her pathway. Hearing of her trials, I thought I would visit her at her school. I therefore called at the village and went to the school house and found it a large brick edifice. I knocked at the door, and Lulu met me in a graceful and

ladylike manner. She offered me a chair upon the
rostrum, but some way I preferred a seat back
among the scholars. I at once was well pleased
with the way she conducted her school. Everything was in order. Wreaths of lovely flowers,
plucked with her own hands, adorned the room.
A motto, "God bless our school," surrounded by a
wreath of clustered grapes and thorns, bleeding-
harts, and pansies, painted with artistic taste,
were there to please the eye. She, as everwhere
else, made sunshine there. I had not been in the
room long before there was another rap at the
door. Lulu stopped and opened the door. A fine
looking young man entered, whom I recognized as
the principal of the institution, having before met
him. He was a noble, intelligent young man.
He took his seat upon the rostrum, and as I sat
opposite him, I read his fine features. Lulu glided
around the room with seraphic grace, her musical
voice swept with cadence through the room. The
look of an angel was on her face, and the room
seemed to be a hallowed place. She heard one
class after another and the scholars seemed to understand well their lessons. The young man's eyes
followed Lulu about the room, and his noble face
lighted up with wild admiration. I then read in
his countenance, words his lips dare not utter.
Why should he utter those words? He the son of
Hon——, who at that time was running for
Governor of the state. He who had been cradled

in the lap of luxury, and a graduate of one of the
leading colleges of the state. She, the daughter
of sorrow, dissipation and misery; she, whose face
had oft been wet with tears she could not repress;
she, who had tried to raise a fallen mother from
the dust, and had spent her wages to take care of
that poor, dissipated mother, who had lost the
faculty of appreciating what was done for her.
"Cast thy bread upon the waters and thou shalt
find it after many days." "Though I walk through
the valley and shadow of death, I will fear no evil,
for Thou art with me; Thy rod and Thy staff, they
shall comfort me." As the young man took his
leave, his remarks were words of commendation,
in regard to the school. "Well, Lulu," said I,
"you have a fine school, and it does me much
good to see how well you are getting along."

"Yes," said Lulu, "I have much to be thankful
for."

———

"I guess," said I to myself, "I will go and make
May a visit, for I expect it nearly killed her when
she heard what Jane had done." Upon arriving
there I said to May, "how are you getting along?"

"I am well; but have you heard how Jane has
been doing?"

At this she broke down weeping, so I really was
afraid her mind might be effected.

"Never mind, May," said I, "no doubt all will
come out right yet."

"But how can dear, darling Lulu stand it to have this great disgrace thrown upon her? Just think of that poor girl with that large school on her hands, and now to face such disgrace!"

"Well," said I, "it may not hurt her as bad as you think it will."

"Yes it will," said May. "We have tried to do everything for Jane that we were able to do, but the more we do for her, the more she expects us to do. You know many of the people in the village know nothing about her. We cannot blame them for thinking very strangely about it. She has plenty to do with, besides if she would go to work and stop gadding the streets and talking about her children she would do much better. I have had so much trouble with her that I have often wished I could die."

"You are discouraged," said I.

"Well, have I not had enough trouble to discourage any one? I have worked hard to raise Lulu, often denying myself of clothing in order to provide for her, and now just in the most important time of her life to think her own mother would try to do everything she can against the lovely girl."

"Well it is a shame. Of course she does it just for spite. She is not very responsible, yet she does know enough to have all of the old tramps she can get running after her. Yes, May, it is too bad. Your folks have had the worst time with that woman of any people I ever knew. If you don't reap your reward in heaven, then I can't understand it, for surely you never can on earth."

"I often think I never would take a child that has one living relative again, but what would become of all of the poor little orphan children that have low relatives if everybody would do in that way? I had to take darling Lulu or the dear girl would have been in her grave, as little Willie is."

"Well," said I, "no doubt she would, but we must try and love those who despitefully use us."

"I do not care what Jane says about me, but to try and disgrace her own lovely daughter, now, as she has just been placed in such a responsible position, is more than I am able to stand. The other day, as I was passing down the street in T——, (this was the place where Lulu was teaching school), Mr. B——, the overseer of the poor, stopped me and inquired if it could be possible that Miss Montroville's mother was suffering? I became so much excited I did not know what to say. I knew Jane had plenty and we had told her if she needed anything to come to us and we would get it for her."

"Oh, well," said I, "it is just one of her tricks. You and her kind brother might give her every cent you both have, and she would be the same careless person she now is; there is no use of caring anything about it, but I realize because of your high-strung organization and sensitive nerves it is almost impossible for you to stand it, and on account of your great love for Lulu who is dearer to you, I do believe, than your own life."

"Yes, she is. I have done just as much for her as I could had she been my own child; besides I have been blamed sometimes because I loved her too much, and other times because I loved her too little. I have been found fault with thousands of times by Jane and her husband. I have been talked about by others because I did not do more for all of them; but all this I can stand. But oh, to think of that lovely girl having to bear all of the gossip that evil persons may cast upon her."

"It is bad enough," said I, "for a girl to have such a mother, but May, you must try and be quiet. It is bad enough, I know, but you can't stand it to worry about it as you do. Try and look to the One that doeth all things well."

CHAPTER XXVII.

I happened to be at one of the societies in the town where Lulu Montroville was teaching. The society was of a benevolent nature, and for the promotion of good. Not long after we were gathered, and had begun our mission of doing good, a Mrs. Hall said, "Oh! have you heard the news?"

"News! what news?" came from a number of women.

"Why, have you not heard it? It's all over town about our teacher letting her mother suffer for food and clothing."

"Yes, I should think we had heard it," said Mrs. Swarts, "and I gist think ef I was in that teacher's place I'd take off some of that finery. Did you see her dress—the one that she had on last week? It was a nice black one. I s'pose, but I dunno, ef I railly had a girl that would treat me as she does her mother, I, wal, I railly dunno what I would do."

"Well," said Mrs. Church, "you have been a different mother to your daughter than Miss Montroville's mother has been to her."

"I don't care ef I have. She is her mother, and a mother is a mother," said Mrs. Swarts.

"Yes, but you know circumstances make a difference, some times."

"I don't care for circumstances. I gist think it is a shame and a disgrace to our town, to allow sich a thing. I am gist goin' to see the school board. We pay the biggest tax of anybody, and I'll give 'em fits about it."

"In some way I feel very sorry," said Mrs. Church, "for this young lady. She is such an innocent, and lady-like appearing girl."

"Oh," said Mrs. Swarts, "you're always feelin' sorry for some one. That is one of your weak points."

"Well," said Mrs. Church, "our teacher is very young, much the youngest of any of the teachers in the school."

"Yes, and that shows what sense the school board had to put such a young thing in that important place," chimed in Mrs. Swarts.

"She is getting along very nicely with her school, is she not?"

"Oh, I guess she is," replied Mrs. Swarts, "but just to think of her lettin' her mother suffer. I met her as I was comin' but I did not speak to her. I am above speakin' to sich a girl."

"Well," said Mrs. Clinton, as she raised her gold-bowed spectacles to wipe away a tear that glistened in her eye, "ladies, I see you're unacquainted with the embarrassments that your young teacher has to encounter. I have known her from her babyhood. I know her to be a pure, noble, lovable young lady. Although she has one awful trial to bear. Her mother is a person of very peculiar character. Not what you might call foolish or crazy. If this were the case then her friends could do something with her, but she is one of those half-witted, silly women, who has no love for her home or children, that no one can do anything with."

At this, chimed in Mrs. Jones, a woman who was somewhat envious of Lulu, and a woman who very much desired to have the young professor admire her daughter, whom she knew to be his equal in family relation, "It is very strange, indeed, if this girl will neglect her own mother. I think a person who would do such a thing as that is not fit to be recognized. What do you think?"

"Well," said Mrs. Clinton, "if such were the case then I should think just as you do, but I know it to be false. This dear, sweet young lady, when only a little, helpless and worse than orphan child, at the death of her father, whom I knew to be a nice, intellectual, young man, was cast out upon a cold world. Her mother neither possessed the love nor the ability to take care of her children, caring more to squander what money she had upon any low tramp that happened to come along."

"Oh, well," said Mrs. Jones, "she is her mother just the same."

"This I will admit is true," said Mrs. Clinton, "but the dear girl never knew a mother's tender love. If I were no more of a mother to my own dear girl than she has been to hers, I would spurn the very idea of being called by that saintly name. The tears have often streamed down this poor girl's pale cheek as she became acquainted with the manner in which her mother was conducting herself. Now, why, I pray, should this young lady be crushed for something she cannot help?"

Fortunately there happened to be a writer of world-wide celebrity present, who was a temporary visitor at the place, and considered a great genius, who in answer to Mrs. Clinton's question said: "Ladies, as I for a number of years have had a good opportunity of seeing much of the world, I have given the subject of the duty of parents to their children much thought. I suppose in your rural towns, where you know but little of sin and vice, the name mother is the sweetest and purest name of earth. I, too, think that name should be honored and adored next to that of the blessed Savior, yet this question has two sides to it. Go with me, if you please, to England, France or China, or many more of the country's of the old world, go into their large cities, or even not so far away; go, if you will, to the metropolis of our own beloved United States, and there I will show you women who bear this saintly title, mother, reeling intoxicated, while little children cling to them crying for bread. Or go, if you please, to the hovels of hell, where the Mother of Harlots and the abominations of the earth dwell. There you will see that this holy name of mother is sometimes not just what it should be. And ye parents provoke not your children to wrath; but bring them up in the fear, nurture and admonition of the Lord."

"Well," said Mrs. Jones, becoming somewhat excited, "I think you're treading on forbidden ground."

"Well," said this distinguished guest, "I can not help it if I am. I make no statement but what I can prove."

"You know," said Mrs. Jones, "the bible says: 'Honor thy father and thy mother, that thy days may be long upon the earth."

"I know so much has been said upon the duty of children to parents that the other side of the matter—the duty of parents to children—has been little noticed; but now, when all social questions are receiving attention, this must soon attract more discussion. I," said the distinguished guest, "should like to hear the lady who said she had been acquainted with your teacher, give a little history of the young lady's mother."

"Well," said Mrs. Clinton, "as I said before, I have known her from her babyhood, and had it not been for her grandma, while she was living, and since that time for her aunt, I am quite sure the dear girl would have long ago been in her grave. She has ever been a frail child. Her aunt has done everything she could to educate and prepare her for society and to make her a blessing to the world. She is one of the most lovable girls I ever knew. Her mother is just the reverse."

"It is imperative," said the author, "that children be from infancy taught obedience and respect to parents, but unless the life of that parent proves a daily demonstration of truths taught, what good the teaching? If a parent, while continually setting forth the duty of parental respect, yet daily performs acts of low and mean degree, how can that child, by any possible stretch of will or imagination, feel the respect for that parent, demanded of him? and who feels wounded if he finds himself not the recipient thereof? It is like pretending that snow is black, when you know it is white."

"The union between Lulu's mother and father, was a sad one," continued Mrs. Clinton. "It was one of those imperfect ties that pass under the name."

"Ah! there it is, how many wretched abodes there are because of such imperfect ties. But I do truly thank God that there are marriages so blessed, the choice so perfect, that the home is a foretaste of eternity."

"Yes, indeed," said Mrs. Clinton, " there are, yet I have often thought it a very merciful thing that the marriages of earth, have no historic effect upon the ties of heaven."

" Well," said the writer, " I firmly take the ground, and am not afraid of successful contradiction, that a parent owes it to a child that he or she shall bring no disgrace upon that child. And his duty in this respect is much more imperative than is that of his child toward him because the parent is the author of the child's life. It is their bounden duty to see to it that their child's life be made just as bright and desirable as possible ; that not only food and shelter and raiment be supplied, that an education and a fair start in life be guaranteed (and every parent owes this to his child, else he should never have been a parent); but also, that there shall never creep into that young heart a doubt of the parent's worth, or a lack of confidence, or a shame for the source of his existence."

" I do firmly believe," said Mrs. Clinton, "that your young teacher's mother, on account of her knowing herself to be the mother of so pure a girl as Lulu is, and possessing not one spark of true motherly affection, does all in her power to disgrace her daughter. I have seen so many of her disgraceful tricks. I stood by and saw the wretchedness which surrounded William, Lulu's father, on every side, and said to myself that if it were possible to utter the impulse of my soul, I would cry throughout the breadth of earth a warning to the haste, or the presumption of an unwise marriage. I happened to be at his house during his last sickness. Oh, if you could have seen the wretchedness that surrounded him. It fairly makes my heart bleed yet."

" I, too," said Mrs. Brown, " have known much of Miss Montroville's mother. I have often seen her meet her daughter in company and turn her head just as far away as she could, so her daughter could get no chance to speak to her, as she well knew Lulu was too much of a lady to meet her mother and be unwilling to speak to her, and would afterwards remark to people, 'do you not think a daughter should respect her mother? but Lulu is above speaking to me. She is so big feeling and stuck up.' This statement, although .strange, is nevertheless true."

" I, too," said Rev. Crawford, " think the subject of training children of vital importance, and that the responsibility of parents, of mothers especially, is almost entirely ignored. You know," said he, " it nearly ruins a young person's name to say that he or she is disrespectful to their mother, because you know Our Maker has conferred upon woman the highest honor ever bestowed upon mortal, and assigned to her the holiest mission that belongs to earth. Yet there is a great difference in mothers. I do feel so very sorry for your young teacher, because I, too, know her to be a most worthy young lady, and I very much fear low and malicious people, on account of a weak and silly mother, will try all they can to mar this pure and innocent girl's name. You know, it is the mother's office to watch over the unfolding intellect, and give bent to the mind; her hand moulds, and gives bent to the character, and she may shape it as she will. To her belongs the incomparable task of fitting immortal souls for their work here, and their eternal destiny hereafter. Yet there are mothers who do not perform their God given work. A parent who really deserves the respect of his children will always receive it, even though darkened by the child's evil deeds; for nature is strong, and filial love is nature. But a parent whose whole life is a round of evil deeds can not expect the respect of his children."

"I do believe," said Mrs. Clinton, "that the world to-day is worse and poorer in great and good men, for the want of more such mothers as were those of John Quincy Adams and John and Charles Wesley, and although terrible denunciation has always attended the ungrateful child, yet I would like to hear a little more said of the wrong acts and faulty teachings of an unworthy parent. I believe that God will not excuse the former, and will visit his wrath far heavier on the parent."

———

"Well my son," said Hon. A———, as he placed his spectacles above his forehead, "I think it high time you were thinking about choosing a wife.

You now are old enough to have a home of your own."

"Well," said the young man, whom we will introduce as the principal of the village high school, "I hardly know about it. I suppose the most folks marry long before they are of my age. But pshaw! whom would I marry?

"Well, my son, I have taken much pains with your education, and it is my wish that you should marry well. You know there is much in blood. I prefer you should look well to whom your wife's ancestors were."

"Well," said the young man, while a blush over-spread his face, "I don't know as it makes any difference whether my wife's grandfather, or great grandfather was a judge of a supreme court or a fiddler."

"Look here, my son," as a grave shadow passed over his face, "you know better than that. There is every thing in blood. You know your mother belonged to an old and aristocratic family. She, as you know, has made a good wife and mother. Now my son, I hope you will not bring disgrace on our family."

"Well, father, I know you have been very kind indeed; now who would you have me marry?"

"Well my son, there is Hannah S——, my dear old friend's daughter, and you know he is worth his thousands."

"Oh father," said the young man, "you are not

so cruel as that, are you? Why, she is as homely as a hedge-hog, and I do not like her. I can surely never think of that."

"My son," said the old man, stamping his foot with emphasis on the floor, "you know not what you are talking about. You well know her ancestors were of the first families of Boston. My heart is set on this marriage. She admires you and you must marry her or not a cent of my money shall you ever have. You know I have spent many hundred dollars on your education."

"Well father, she is not educated, and you are aware that she cares nothing about improvement and culture."

"My son, it makes no difference about a woman being educated, only so she can cook, iron, wash, and mend your clothes; you surely know she belongs to an old and wealthy family."

"What do I care about her family. I think for a marriage to prove a happy one minds should blend together. How, I would ask, could a cultured person be happy, married to a very ignorant person?"

"My son, has not blood anything to do with it? If your wife's ancestors are of an old and wealthy family I shall be happy; if not, I shall go to my grave in sorrow. Now, my son, look well before you leap. The first great, important step to consider is good blood, and the next is money."

"Why father, how you talk! How perfectly

cruel!" At this the young man sprang to his feet
and began walking the floor as if in terrible
agony.

"My son," said the old man, "what on earth is
the matter with you? You act as if you were
going crazy. I fear you have placed your affections on some poor girl of common birth. Oh, my
son, you whom I have idolized, to come to such a
fate as this! Rather would I see you laid in your
grave."

"Father, do not talk so. Is there any harm in
loving a pure, noble, intelligent girl, one who has
striven hard to make her life a success?"

"My son, you must not address me thus. I said,
and now I say it again, you shall not bring disgrace upon our family. You shall look at the
ancestors of your wife. Now do not be foolish.
You know Hannah belongs to an old and respectable family."

At this remark of the old gentleman the young
man left the house looking sad and discouraged.

"What a fool," muttered the old man, "a boy
can make of himself. Just let him talk to me
again of a pure, cultured girl!"

———

Dear Lulu, although loved by all who were not
envious of her, yet at the close of her school,
shrunk from the idea of again facing the gaze of
the gossiping town. "I cannot again," said she,
"think of teaching this school. You know there

are many who know nothing of the sorrow that
has always been my lot, on account of the peculiarities of my mother. Strange, strange indeed, to
those who have known a mother's tender care and
protection to see my mother going up and down
the streets reeling and intoxicated, talking about
me. Oh, for a mother's love, a love for some
cause withheld from me."

"God alone this secret can unfold, Lulu. Indeed it has ever been a mystery to me, why you,
so young, so pure, so gentle, should know such
sorrow. But no doubt the change you are about
to make will be for your own good."

"Oh, said May, as she wrung her hands with
grief, how can I give my precious Lulu up? And
yet I know," said she, "if Lulu goes, as she in-
tends, to her uncle's, it will be better for her. He
has ever been kind to her. I know he will protect
her from the vile gossip that has been so unjustly
circulated about her in regard to her mother. I
would not, I could not give her up, did I not think
it for her own good. Her uncle has wealth, while
I have not. He is a good, noble gentleman, and
will gladly shield her good name from slanderous
tongues. She will be the niece of an influential
merchant. You know the child protected with
wealth and influence has many advantages over
one that is not."

"Yes," said I, "they are, yet you remember the
Lord answered Job out of the whirlwind, and said,

'Wilt thou also disannul my judgment? Deck thyself now with majesty and excellency, and array thyself with glory. Look on every one that is proud, and bring him low; and tread down the wicked in their place, then will I confess unto thee that thine own right hand can save.' And you remember that the Lord blessed the latter end of Job's life more than the beginning."

" Yes, indeed, I too think it best for Lulu to go to her uncle, because I know she can do nothing with her mother, and the name of a girl is easily marred."

Lulu felt relieved when her things were ready, and she stood waiting in the little railway station for the train that was to carry her away. Oh, my heart bled for her as I held her hand in mine, and looked into those large and expressive eyes, wet with tears. Oh, how I breathed a prayer that the God of the orphan would protect her, and although sad as I was at the parting, yet I deemed the step she was going to take one that would free her from the many trials she daily had to encounter. Although a lovely girl of some twenty summers, yet Lulu knew much of sorrow. As I took her hand I could scarcely restrain the impulse to lay my head upon her shoulder and have a hearty cry; and although a sweet smile wreathed her rosy lips, and her eyes beamed so lovingly upon me, yet I noticed the tears trembling upon those dear drooping lashes. Other friends bid Lulu farewell, but the dear girl showed no outburst of grief; mild, pure, gentle, as she ever had been, yet she said, "do not think my love for you all will ever change in the least, even if I should stay for many years." I well knew that her words were true, because I knew she was too noble a girl to let either wealth or position make any difference in her affections toward those she loved. Oh, how the tears flowed down May's face after Lulu had bid her adieu.

"Well," said I, "May you had better return home and I will see Lulu on the train. I saw that May was so overcome with grief that it would be much better for her not to see Lulu get on the train."

"Well," said Lulu, "You must write to me."

"Yes, indeed, dear girl, I will, for I am anxious to know how you get along."

As the train came hurrying in that would bear dear Lulu to the far away western city where she was going, a father and his son were also awaiting its arrival.

"So you are going away, are you Miss Montroville?" said the father.

"Yes," said Lulu, I am going to my uncle's with whom I lived a short time when a little girl."

"I understand he is your mother's brother."

"Yes," said Lulu.

As the old gentleman was also going a number of miles westward he turned to bid his son good by, and was greatly surprised to find him so overcome he could hardly speak. The young man cast a hurried look at Lulu without a parting word. Ah! Why could he not take her hand in his and say a last farewell? Ah! the trouble was the distance between them was too great. He, the son of influence and luxury; she, the daughter of sorrow, ignorance, and misery. She, whose cheeks had often been wet with tears she could not suppress; she, who had known much of bitter sorrow and affliction.

"Well," remarked the old gentleman somewhat nervously to a friend he happened to meet on the train, "that young Miss Montroville, who taught in the same school of which my son was the principal, is a rather charming girl, is she not?"

"Yes," said his friend, "one of the finest girls I ever saw. But the poor girl has many things to contend with that are very hard to bear."

"Well," said the old gentleman," what fools some young folks can make of themselves. Talk to me about culture and improvement. What does it all amount to unless a person belongs to a good family? Sir, there is much in blood."

"Well, sir," said his friend, "I believe a child that works its way up in the world with every difficulty to surmount is just as deserving as one that is surrounded with every blessing of life. Look at the illy arranged families in our country. Look at the hundreds of thousands of helpless little children that have no advantages at all."

Shortly after Lulu went away, there began to be a change in the actions of the young professor. He began to sink into a melancholy state of mind. The doctors said he had nervous prostration. His father was summoned back from the west, very much worried about his son's health. The best medical skill could do nothing, and he gradually sunk into a deranged state of mind, and before many months filled a premature grave. His father was crushed at the death of his son, and life to him became only a burden. "Why," said he, "was my noble boy taken from me? He was my only hope and joy." The gray locks and stooped form of the old man told too true that his heart was broken, and that before many months he would follow his son.

CHAPTER XXVIII.

Not long after Lulu went away, I happened to be visiting in the west; and, as I had a friend who lived in the same city where her uncle resided, I thought I would visit there. I thought to myself I will not let Lulu know I am so near her. Shortly after my arrival my friend and I were walking along one of the fine drive ways, when presently there passed us an elegant carriage with prancing horses, driven by a coachman. It was one of the finest surreys I ever saw. Turning to me my friend said, " there goes the beautiful and accomplished niece of Mr. W——, one of our enterprising merchants. I understand she is an orphan, and has come to reside with her uncle." As I glanced at the carriage .my heart gave a bound, for who should I see but my dear young friend Lulu. As I had made up my mind not to let Lulu know of my arrival, I said, " indeed, a very fine carriage." Then my friend went on to say, " she must be a very fine young lady to be the niece of so worthy a gentleman as he."

"No doubt," said I. But at the same time I could not help thinking, is the dear girl any better than she was when looked upon as the daughter of a poor dissipated mother? I said to myself, no doubt, to the eyes of the world she is, but not to God.

"Yes," said my friend, " blood will tell."

" No doubt it will," said I, "in some cases, but as I have given the subject much thought I have made up my mind that it surely does not in every case." I noticed my friend looked very much astonished to think I did not agree with him on the subject, so I said no more, and we changed our conversation. On the following Sunday I attended one of the large and fashionable churches with my friend. We had not been seated long before in walked Lulu, escorted by a fine looking gentleman, whom I afterward learned was a relative of her's, and the chorister of the church. He proudly led her up the choir. I noticed that she passed up the aisle with the same unaffected ease that she did in the little church near her childhood's home. I noticed that all eyes were bent on the lovely girl, partly, no doubt, on account of her being a stranger and partly on account of her unaffected ease and beauty. I was almost overcome with rapture as I caught the sound of her fine alto voice as it floated through those magnificent halls. I was glad that my friend's pew was situated where I was unnoticed by Lulu, though I could plainly see her. The dear girl was richly clad. Those same large, expressive eyes, instead of being wet with tears were sparkling with beauty, and there was a mild and happy expression on her face. After the service closed, and we were on our way home, my friend said to me, " what a very fine singer that strange young lady is who sang to-day in the choir. She is, I understand, a near relative of the chorister. I knew he referred to Lulu, so feeling anxious to learn who the gentleman was that accompanied Lulu, I said, " who was the gentleman with the strange young lady whom you refer to?"

" Oh," said my friend, " that was Prof. W——, one of the finest singers in the city. We are invited to attend a large party given in honor of this young lady next week."

I could not help feeling very glad of the invitation as I very much desired to watch the difference in the attention paid to one who was looked upon as a relative of influential people, or one who was thought to belong to people not so worthy. Indeed, the difference was very surprising. At the party dear Lulu was admitted to be the belle of the evening. All did homage to her, and she was looked upon as a very accomplished and worthy young lady, which indeed she was. But nevertheless was she really any better than when her face was wet with tears, when the frown of a whole community was upon her for something she could no more help or change than she could the laws of gravitation? Oh, if we could go into the wretched houses and see the sorrow there, I do believe it would give us a missionary spirit, and a determ-

17

ination to go out into the world and labor there.

As my stay in the city necessarily had to be short, I left Lulu there surrounded with wealth and friends, the same pure, innocent girl she had ever been. In Ward Montroville's home, beautiful sons and daughters have grown up. His oldest daughter is attending one of the leading colleges of the state. Charlie has grown almost to manhood, a bright and noble boy. As no little ones have ever come to gladden the heart and home of May and her husband, there then was a vacant chair that Lulu alone could fill, who was indeed the music and the sunshine of their home. " Sing, O heavens, and be joyful, O earth, for the Lord hath comforted his people, and will have mercy upon his afflicted." " Can a woman forget her sucking child? Yea, they may forget, yet I will not forget thee, saith the Holy One of Israel."

———

While attending one of the most successful universities of the United States, Lulu became acquainted with a young man whom we will call Wilmot Haverland, a young man of fine mental ability, who was taking a course in Law. He was of commanding appearance, over six feet tall, very handsomely built, with high, noble forehead, and keen blue eyes, which bespoke more than ordinary intellect. He soon became perfectly enchanted with the pure, noble girl. Naturally too intelli-

gent to criticise Lulu's ancestry, he did everything to ennoble the girl whom he hoped to secure
as his wife. Their friendship rapidly developed,
and before many months passed he proudly led
Lulu to the altar, bedecked in handsome array.
He looked into the pure, sweet face of her whom
he honored above all others as his bride, and in a
few moments the clergyman pronounced them
man and wife. He soon found out that he had
made a wise choice. Lulu, in her own home as
elsewhere, was a constant beam of sunshine. Mr.
Haverland soon became one of the most successful
lawyers in his state, and his young wife was all he
asked for, as she knew well how to oversee her
household. In due time other joys came to their
home, the voice of a baby boy, first delighted the
hearts of the young parents, and before many
years passed a little daughter with its mother's
beautiful eyes, and her sunny disposition, came to
add more happiness to their home. And now, just
before we let the curtains fall over their home we
will just take one other peep. A well arranged
household with all of the modern improvements;
a large, spacious lawn with flowers of the most
rare and gorgeous hue; horses, and carriages with
colored servants and waiters of the most trained
and obedient kind, and sitting on the bench of the
Supreme Court, Judge Haverland, the once promising young lawyer, is now the admiration of his
native land.

CHAPTER XXIX.

In a quiet country graveyard, where the gentle zephyrs play among the leaves, sweetly sleeps the body of William Montroville, with his father and mother by his side. Here every year do comrades, those brave and gallant men, that faced the cannon's deadly mouth, who have united heart and hand to once a year strew flowers over the graves of their comrades, who stood the hardships of a long and bloody war, meet, and with loving hands place flowers and the beautiful stars and stripes over William's grave, little knowing the whole of his history. Although obscure and unknown, yet may he sweetly sleep with God's blessing upon him ; and although his young and useful life was blighted here, in this world of sin and sorrow, yet he sleeps with our nation's beautiful emblem waving over his grave. That same flag which he loved so much, and which he saw used as a bed quilt in the old southern planter's house, while acting as a spy away down in the sunny south, the sight of which made his warm blood boil :

Strew flowers o'er me, comrades brave,
While you are marching near.
It would be more pleasant in the grave,
If I could know you placed them here.

Place those dear flags, one at my head,
　Another at my feet,
That they may wave tho' I am dead;
　To me they were complete.

Oh, may you see those colors float,
　Their beauty is so rare,
On land on spire, 'mid sea on boat,
　And through the azure air.

You well remember comrades dear,
　Upon that awful day,
The distant battle wail sound clear,
　We thought our lives we'd pay.

Upon a fort a flag there waved,
　Our colonel saw it there,
'Mid death he rushed our flag to save,
　While lightning filled the air.

He tore it from its lofty stand,
　And placed our colors there.
He bravely waved it in his hand,
　Then threw it to the air.

Upon that dreaded battlefield,
　Where blood ran fast and deep,
You bravely said you would not yield,
　Tho' the last sleep you'd sleep.

Oh, may those stars wave over your grave,
　When you are sleeping low,
We fought and bled, them for to save,
　We could not let them go.

A Wife's and Husband's Mistake.

CHAPTER I.

At one of our summer resorts a young man of quiet and amiable disposition spent much time with a young woman, who was the daughter of very indulgent parents, who had indulged their child in having her own way about almost every-thing. The young man was drawn into her company, or at least was always devising plans to be with the young lady, whom we will call Mildred Hawthorne. He no doubt felt at times that the hasty, impulsive girl, was not the one fitted to make for him a happy home, but led on by that strange inclination or infatuation that often unites in the holy bond of wedlock those so illy mated, who could never agree just exactly on one subject, or see things in just the same light. Strange that there should be any possible chance for people to make such a mistake, to marry and drag out a miserable life.

After a somewhat disagreeable courtship, Mark Allen married the wayward Mildred Hawthorne, and took her to his quiet country home. Now Mark was one of those good, quiet persons, that little of this world's goods will satisfy; but Mil·

dred was proud and ambitious and very hard to
suit.

"Well, Mildred," said Mark shortly after they
had begun housekeeping, " I am going this afternoon down to Willton," this was a small town a
few miles distant, "would you not like to accom-
pany me ?"

Mildred was just finishing her ironing, and felt
somewhat proud of her success in her first attempt
in doing up a nice lot of fine linen shirts for her
husband. "Yes," she said, " I would like very
much to go. We can take tea with your sister
Nellia. But Mark, you must change your shirt,"
giving a glance at the nice, pure, white shirts
which she had taken so much pains to do up.

"No, I am in a hurry ; this shirt is good enough,
besides, what is the use? I am a married man
and my market is made."

"Then I shall not go, for you look like a fright."

"Well then, you will have to stay at home,"
said he, as he jumped into his buggy and drove off.
"I am not going to be bothered with all of her
silly whims," thought Mark, as he half regretfully
hastened on his way.

"He never once noticed how hard I have
worked," thought Mildred, as she laid her head on
her ironing table and began to cry; "but I just
would not go with him with that old dirty shirt on,
I just wanted him to plainly understand that."
Mildred sat pouting for some time, then got up

saying, "I guess he will understand I am not going with him when he has on a dirty shirt."

Mark drove as quickly as possible to the village, never stopping to take tea with his sister, and after forgetting half he had intended to purchase, started home half sorry that he had not taken time to change his shirt so his wife would have accompanied him. He well knew she had worked hard, and of course the change would have done her good, besides, they could have taken tea and spent the time pleasantly with his sister; " but," thought he, " we now are married, and such foolishness will not do. I look well enough."

Poor Mildred, as the shades of night began to gather, was feeling quite lonely. " Oh, dear!" said she, " what shall I do? He may not come home to night. I have offended him, and I may have to stay alone. Oh, dear, what shall I do? She hurried around, did up the chores, and then after getting a nice dainty supper, setting the table with snowy cloth, arranging the silver and China dishes with more than usual neatness, sat down to await her husband's arrival; but there was an unusual throbbing of her heart and a keen aching pain piercing her breast, as she awaited his return.

Mark, too, was quite nervous, and thought the road never before so long. " Oh, dear, if anything should happen her; but then it will not do to indulge her pride, or give up in small things. Married folks must use judgment. ' Pride always goes before a fall.' "

Mildred had almost given up his return. She now began to walk the floor while tears flowed down her cheeks. At last the sound of a buggy driven at rapid speed, but quite a distance off, caught her ear. How gladly those sounds fell on her ear. Her first impulse was to rush to her husband and throw her arms around him and express her happiness in words of tender love and ask his forgiveness. But no, that would not be womanly; it would be too humiliating, so she simply said, "What on earth kept you so long?"

"I guess I can stay just as long as I wish when I go to town," said Mark.

CHAPTER II.

The next morning, both Mildred and her husband were much more attentive to the desires of each other. Mildred indeed possessed a very tender love for her husband, yet on account of her headstrong disposition enjoyed having her own way. Mark, no doubt, also possessed a tender regard for the wishes of his wife, whom he knew also wished her own way; but his was a stubborn will, and when he once said a thing he meant it; if he said he was going to do a thing he did it, and it made no difference what his wife wished or cared. At one time Mildred wished to attend a gathering of young people. Now parties, sociables and picnics, were places Mark did not enjoy. Mildred was all excitement over the anticipated gathering, thinking of course Mark would go.

"Oh, Mark, there is going to be a party at Mr. Hawthorn's, will you not go?"

"No," said Mark, "I never enjoy parties, and I am not going."

"Oh, please do go," said Mildred, "I do so wish to go. All of the young folks will be there."

"Well, it makes no difference to me, I am not going, I do not enjoy parties. You can go without me."

"Well, stay if you wish, I am not going to stay at home like some old woman." So off went Mildred, saying to herself, "dear me, I do wish Mark would go, I would so enjoy having him with me. I know I will not have half as good a time, besides I am so ashamed to be seen without my husband so soon after marriage. I expect I should have stayed with him, but I do not intend to always stay at home, and just as one begins they will have to do."

Mark spent the evening at home all alone, feeling somewhat provoked at his wife. I do not intend to be running around to every fool party; they are no places for me, besides, I intend to have my own way, thought Mark. After whittling, and whistling a somewhat lonesome tune, Mark retired to bed and was soon fast asleep. Mildred missed her husband very much, but was determined not to let those present see that she was embarrassed because he was not with her.

"Well, Mildred," said Nettie Gleason, "where is Mark?"

"At home, of course."

"Oh, such a droll fellow, he never enjoyed young people's company; but Mildred, if I were you I would just let him stay at home. I would not begin to indulge him in having his own way."

At this, Mrs. Hawthorn, the lady of the house and a person of broad observation, joined the conversation. "Well, girls," said she, "I am much older than either of you, and have had a sad experience in my life. I would like to say just one word here. There is great danger in this having one's own way. I would advise this young lady to try and overlook the peculiarities of her husband, and try and humor him all she can. I tell you there is danger in having our own way."

At this remark of Mrs. Hawthorn a crimson flush passed over Mildred's cheek. The party had lost its charms for her, and she hastily put on her wraps and excusing herself hurried home. Her husband was sleeping soundly, so Mildred quietly crept in bed feeling half ashamed for leaving him alone. She very much desired her husband's forgiveness, yet was too proud to let him know of her anxiety. How glad she would have been if he had asked her if she was not sorry. But this Mark would never do, so there began to be a little coldness springing up between them. Mark's business was of such a character that he was often called to a distant city. He being a fine business man, made rapid bargains, and success in financial matters was fast giving him a good reputation as a shrewd speculator. Of course women like Mildred felt very proud of her husband's success, and at first did everything to encourage him on towards making money. She was very anxious to have a better home than the one Mark had first taken her to. Mark was well satisfied with the plain home, but his wife's proud, ambitious disposition had awakened a desire in him to get money so he could supply her every desire. He began at first to buy while away in the city fine presents to please his wife. As soon as he possibly could he built him a nice, new house. This was just what Mildred desired. She now, more anxious than ever before, began to worry, first for one nice new piece of furniture, and then another. Almost every time Mark came from the city he brought home some nice, new piece of furniture. But poor, silly Mildred had now become so proud and foolish that nothing was half nice enough for her.

"Why, Mark," she would say, "did you get this, it is not just what I wanted, Mrs. Dean has one much nicer."

"Well, I thought this would suit you."

"But it does not," said Mildred.

The next time Mark went to the city Mildred said, "now Mark, I want you to get me a new secretary. Now, this time I want you to do your best in the selection, for you are so liable to make mistakes."

"I will do the best I can," said Mark, and so he did.

"I do hope this time I can please her. It does seem to me that nothing will suit her. Mark had now become quite nervous, being continually drummed to death, first about one thing then another, and his patience was nearly gone, but he thought once again he would try to suit his wife.

He bought one of the best secretaries he could find, thinking "surely this will suit her." But just as soon as poor, foolish Mildred saw it, she exclaimed, "For mercy sake! Why, Mark, did you get this? It is not what I wanted at all. Dear me, I always did hate a fool, and surely that is just what you are."

At this Mark left the house exclaiming, "Well, after this you must do your own selecting."

"Why Mildred," said Tinna Geld, a young lady who was visiting at Mildred's, and for whom Mildred would have done almost anything, "I am sorry you spoke so to Mark. I saw it hurt him very much, besides I do not see how you could not be pleased. This is surely one of the nicest and best secretaries I ever saw."

"Oh, I know it is, and I am sorry too, but you know it is just my way of speaking," said Mildred.

"Yes, but it will not always do to be so abrupt."

Mark again soon went to the city. He now

began to lose the love for his home he no doubt would have felt had his wife treated him more tenderly, and had she tried harder to have been pleased with the things he bought for her. While away in the city he boarded at a fashionable hotel. There were ladies whom he associated with; one, a handsome young widow, who was perfectly infatuated with the " shrewd young speculator," as she called Mark. She possessed a forward disposition, and did everything to make a good impression upon Mark.

" Well, Mr. Allen," said she, " you must be very lonely away from home. Why not come into the parlor and spend your evenings with us ?" At this request Mark smoothed his dark mustache, giving it an extra curl. As thoughts of Mildred at home came into his mind, a dark blush overspread his handsome face. " But," thought he, " she does not care for me, what harm can there be in my spending the evening with other ladies ? I have a mind of my own and I know it is my own business." So Mark passed the evening with the handsome Mrs. Dewey. " Oh," said she, " Mr. Allen, how perfectly delighted I am to have you help me drive dull care away."

" I am so lonely away from home and my business is so I have to spend my time mostly away among strangers."

" It is seldom I meet a person so perfectly entertaining as you are Mr. Allen."

Mark looked into her dark eyes, little dreaming
of the danger there was in so doing. When the
night was far spent and Mark was about to take
his departure, why was it that he so tenderly
pressed the hand so lovingly placed in his?

" You will surely call again, Mr. Allen," said
she.

" Indeed I should be pleased to do so, but I have
business that calls me home to-morrow."

" Oh please wait just one more day; please, I
am so lonely," said the dashing widow.

Again taking her hand which she now extended
in a very affectionate way, Mark answered, " If it
is possible I may stay just one day longer."

As Mark went to his room he could not help
thinking of his wife at home whom he knew
would be greatly displeased if she knew of his
spending his evenings with another lady. " But,"
thought he, "she will never know it, and what
harm can there be in passing the time as pleasantly as possible? But I guess I had better go
home to morrow. I know Mildred will be very
anxious about me, but she is so disagreeable I can
hardly stand it with her. Still she is my wife, she
works hard and keeps everything nice and tidy.
But her everlasting tongue I just despise. If she
could only be pleasant and cheerful like Mrs.
Dewey. But she naturally has such an unpleasant disposition, I expect she cannot help." The
next morning Mark arose, feeling a desire to go

home. He knew very well it was the place for him, but thoughts of the handsome young widow were constantly before him. Oh, how perfectly charming is her company, if Mildred was only half so agreeable he felt that he should be glad to go home. As the hours passed quickly by he said to himself, "I never cared so much about staying away from home before, but Mildred is so unpleasant that I dread to go home, and I can stay just as well as not. What harm can there be when I can pass the evening so pleasantly here? So he staid and again spent the evening in the parlor with Mrs. Dewey. How quickly the hours passed away! Mrs. Dewey was one of those dashing women who flatters with her tongue, and drags men down to the gates of hell. She knew from the first that Mark greatly admired her. She also knew that he was just the one to draw on by her cunning devices. He had plenty of money and was away from home and lonely. She being a fine musician stepped to the piano, and as her skillful fingers swept the keys of the instrument, and her child-like voice floated through the room on the midnight air, from the impulse of the moment or a spell he could not overcome, Mark sprang to her side and caught her frail form in his arms and kissed her ruby lips over and over again, pressed her to his heart, and then recovering for a moment he thought, "My God! what have I done?" But it was too late. The spell he could not break, and

18

he held the willing, beguiling, treacherous woman to his heart. "My blessed Savior," breathed he, "what have I done? But it is too late; my heart belongs to this handsome woman."

We will leave them alone with their guilt.

This very night Mark fell as deep in sin as it is possible for a married man to fall in pressing a strange woman to his breast.

At Mark Allen's home there was a different scene. Mildred walked the floor and wrung her hands with grief for there seemed to come to her some awful forebodings of evil. "Why, oh why, does Mark not come?" Tears streamed down her blanched cheeks. Oh, that her unborn babe that knew so little of its mother's grief, was born, to bring new charms to the home of this unhappy wife and husband. But before the little one ever opened its eyes to behold the light of this beautiful world, the young mother was so overcome with grief and anxiety and her nervous system became so exhausted and weak, that while Mark was absent on one of his long visits to the city, enjoying the society of the strange woman, she gave premature birth to her little one. Kind hands of loving friends dressed the little one for its long resting place. Poor Mildred pressed the little form of her dead baby to her breast and said, "Oh, if Mark would only come!" But he now had fallen so low that he did not care anything at all for his home, often staying weeks, and sometimes months, always making an excuse that it was business detained him. Upon this occasion it was impossible to find him, so the little one was quietly laid to rest in the cemetery near Mildred's home. Mildred's life was almost despaired of for some time. When Mark returned home he felt very much displeased with his wife. He said she had no business to worry about him; she might have known he was able to take care of himself, and he hardly went into the room to see her. Mildred was so weak and exhausted she could scarcely raise her head, but so glad to see her husband that when he came near her she begged him to come to her. She took his hand in hers and drew him to her and kissed him over and over again. Mark looked at his once beautiful wife, but now her beauty was faded and gone. He stooped down and kissed her pale lips, but all love for his faded wife was gone. He thought only of the beautiful, charming young widow who had won his heart. So he soon made an excuse that his business was such he must go to the city again.

CHAPTER III.

Mildred slowly recovered so as to be able to sit up for a little while at a time, but there was a loneliness hovering around her she could not shake off. Her husband now hardly ever came home to stay more than one or two days at a time, and

when he did he was so cross and absent-minded
that he was no company for her at all. Poor Mildred knew that his love for her was gone, and she
tried in every way possible to win him back, but
it was impossible for her to do so. She was so
weak and discouraged that life was a burden.
Gladly would she have given her life for the love
of her companion. She spent hours and hours at
home alone. Her mental suffering was so great,
and her nervous system so racked, that in an hour
of despondency she tried to take her own life.
Every little thing annoyed her husband. Their
beautiful and well ordered home had no attraction for him. He had fallen so low that he would
tell his friends that their home for him was a pandemonium. The servants annoyed him and had no
patience with any one or anything. At every little
annoyance he would curse and swear so that Mildred was constantly in fear that something would
displease him. He now scarcely ever spoke a kind
word to his wife, and appeared to fairly hate the
very sight of her. One day some little thing happened to annoy him, and he rushed to the house,
hardly dressed himself, and started away. Mildred, very much frightened, and hardly daring to
speak, followed him to the door and said, "Mark,
where are you going?"

"It makes no difference to you, where I am
going. You go into the house and mind your own
business. You always wanted to run things, and

now you can have the privilege." Mildred sank half fainting to the floor. She felt that the climax had been reached. She felt a foreboding of some awful calamity she could not tell what. Alone, faint and sick, she wept until tears failed to come. With a ghastly look and racked brain, she arose from the floor, wrung her hands, and a look of despair overspread her face. Then she gradually sank into a long nervous sick-spell. The name of her husband was constantly on her lips as she rolled in wild delirium on her bed.

At the depot Mark took the first train west, telling some of his friends that he was going to leave home never to return.

"Why," said a friend, a man who had known Mildred from her babyhood, "you must surely go back home and tell your wife what you are going to do. It will kill her to leave her so."

"No, I am not going back. My home is a hell for me, and I hope I will never see it again." So the fast express soon bore him many miles from his home.

Mildred's friends and neighbors, as soon as they had heard what Mark had done, and that he was gone, came to her assistance. They very kindly and gently sympathized with her. They tried to make her believe that her husband would soon return. They did every thing to restore her to life again.

Oh, how Mildred prayed to die. Life without

her husband was a misery. But as it is not always possible for one to die when they most want to, Mildred slowly recovered; her frail nature could stand more than one would think. But she merely lived because she could not die; her home had forever lost its charms to her. She constantly thought, "is Mark living, or is he dead?"

As soon as Mark was far enough from home so that he supposed no one would know what he was doing, he sat down and wrote a letter to the dashing Mrs. Dewey, as follows: "I cannot live without you. Come to me, and we will go to a distant city and pass the remainder of our lives together." Mrs. Dewey was very much pleased. She thought, "this is a good chance for me. Mr. Allen has lots of money, and I can spend my life in ease." She hastily arranged her wardrobe, dressed in gorgeous array, and set sail for her distant lover.

Mark, after securing large, spacious rooms to receive his unlawful paramour, anxiously awaited her arrival. The artful, treacherous woman well knew how to beguile him. As long as Mark's money lasted they were apparently happy. He did everthing for this deceitful woman that money could do. Dressed her in the most gorgeous clothing, and hired servants of the most obedient kind, so that her fair jeweled hands should keep their snowy whiteness. But as it is impossible for those who doeth evil to prosper: Romans, 13–4: But if thou do that which is evil, be afraid; for he bear-eth not the sword in vain; for he is the minister of God, a revenger to execute wrath upon him that doeth evil." Mark soon found that his money was fast going to the four winds. He of course had access to the home which Mildred and he had worked so hard to make beautiful, but having a little spark of the feelings left which he once possessed, he could not bear to think of mortgaging the home where he had left Mildred. Neither could he dare to tell the dashing Mrs. Dewey that his money was nearly gone. Then he began to run in debt here and there, at every place possible where he could get money. At last the crisis came. Nobody would let him have one more cent. What to do he did not know. At last things got into such shape that he had to make known to the treacherous woman that they would have to dispense with their servants. At this announcement the gay woman said, "you need not think I will stay with you if your money is gone. There are too many men just like you, whose wealth I am perfectly free to enjoy if I but say the word, so either mortgage your home, and get money, or else say good-by to me forever." This guilty woman had got such control over Mark that he would spend the last cent he had in the world to satisfy her extravagant desires. So he mortgaged his beautiful home where Mildred was, and again for many months he gratified every desire of the vain woman.

Poor Mildred, when notified that their home, their once beautiful and happy home, would soon pass into the hands of others, rallied to the emergency. Having some money left her by her father, she said, "I cannot give up the dear old home." Suffering the most awful mental pain, almost to distraction, she worked and toiled, taking care of the horses, cattle, hogs, assisted only by a young boy and girl. Oh, she would say, "I must save the home, for may be Mark will sometime come back to me." Tears would stream down her faded cheeks, and long into the wee small hours of the night would she walk the floor, and watch the clock, and think, "oh, if he would only come home to me, I would forgive him for all. Will he never come?"

CHAPTER IV.

As soon as Mark's money was gone, the heartless wicked Mrs. Dewey began to accept the attention of other wealthy men. This almost distracted Mark. In his sober moments he would say, "Oh, if I had not been so stubborn, and had humored the peculiar disposition of my own dear wife, I now might be happy; but I have forsaken my wife, my unborn child, home and honor, all are gone, and now, when my money is all spent, she turns from me; this Mildred would never have done. Why, oh why, did I not see before it was too late?" "But," stamping his foot down, "I will yet have my revenge on this woman who has wrought my ruin."

Mark had now fallen so low that he began to frequent different houses of ill fame, and although almost loathing the inmates, yet dissipation had brought him so low that all self-respect was gone. One night as he was wandering through one of the streets in Chicago, and was passing one of the gilded dens of infamy which rob men of all self-respect and blast all their hopes of eternity, he saw the wicked Mrs. Dewey clasped in the arms of a red, bloated-faced man, whom he knew to be a millionaire. This so enraged the half-crazy Mark that he rushed into the house, caught the wicked woman by the hair, and was dragging her out of the room, when, quick as thought, the burly, red-faced man drew a revolver and fired, accidentally piercing the wicked woman through the heart, and inflicting a mortal wound in Mark's breast. For a few moments everything was excitement. The burly, cowardly, red faced man, as soon as he saw what he had done, fled. In a few moments the police were summoned and poor Mark was taken to a hospital near by, the blood pouring from his breast. His past life unrolled like a scroll before his gaze. His quiet, beautiful country home; his faithful, although peculiar wife; the one he had sworn to honor and love above all others, came up before his dying gaze. The skillful surgeon knew the wound was of such a nature that Mark must die.

19

" Tell me true," said Mark, " must I die ?"

" You are mortally wounded," said the surgeon. " Have you no friends you would like to see ?"

" Yes," said Mark, as the blood ran from the wound, " send for my wife' whom I have for-saken. I know she will come; send for her."

As quickly as the message could be written it was sent over the wire, " Come to Chicago, to No. — street, *for I am dying.* Mark."

Poor Mildred did not stop to arrange any costly wardrobe, but with faded face and plain attire, went as fast as the fast express could carry her to the bedside of her dying husband.

Poor Mark, as soon as she arrived, held up his hands, saying : " forgive me, I am dying."

As Mildred folded her dying husband in her arms, she wet his face with tears. She held him long in her arms and prayed that God would for-give them both. Kneeling by his bed she poured out her soul in prayer, and as tears streamed down her poor, pale cheeks, Mark said : " Hark! the an-gels are calling me ! Oh my Savior is so precious to me ! I hear his gentle voice ! I am forgiven !" and thus he died.

As soon as arrangements could be made, Mildred with the remains of her husband, started to their own country home. Friends were notified. But true to her womanly instincts, Mildred knew it would do no good, that the true cause of her hus-band's murder should be known, so she only said that he was shot by some unknown man, who fled as soon as he had committed the crime.

Mildred had the casket that contained the remains of her once beloved husband taken to their own spacious house, and surrounded by weeping friends the last sad rite was said; then Mark was quietly laid to rest in the cemetery near his home.

The wicked Mrs. Dewey, who had forsaken her own purity and virtue and wasted her youth and beauty; who had broken up homes that might have been happy, and lived in wickedness with men whom she cared nothing for, only to get their money, was taken, as soon as a rough box was procured, and without one friend to shed a tear, was buried in the potter's field.

Mildred, although her heart was broken, and her confidence in humanity gone, yet the God who had sustained her during every earthly sorrow was still her God, and she found his words true, "I will be a father to the fatherless, and the *widow's God.*"